ABOUT THE AUTHOR

D0915491

GUY HOWARD

. . . is the internationally known author of the best sellers, "Walkin' Preacher of the Ozarks" and "Give Me Thy Vineyard"

. . . has walked an average of 4,000 miles a year in the Ozark hills for the past 20 years

. . . has averaged $14.00 a month "salary"

. . . has served dozens of pastorless communities in the Ozark area as pastor, teacher, music director and general advisor on matters of every description

. . . is a familiar and beloved figure in the hills he loves

. . . is distinguished as an author, entertainer, lecturer, humorist, traveler, teacher, preacher and Christian gentleman.

Wings of the Dawn

Wings OF THE Dawn

GUY HOWARD
"the Walkin' Preacher of the Ozarks"

Zondervan Publishing House
GRAND RAPIDS, MICHIGAN

Printed in the United States of America

To My Daughters
Virginia, Louise and Freida

chapter 1

CARRYING A LARGE SUITCASE in each hand,
John Malcom Smith shoved the door open wide
with a mighty push and strode into the half empty
waiting room of the bus depot. He wore a business
suit, finely tailored and of unmistakably good cloth,
but his shirt was tieless and unbuttoned at the
throat. His hat was set at a rakish angle; a wisp of
brown hair covered his forehead.

His entrance awakened the interest of the
listless patrons, bored and unhappy with their long
hours of waiting. No doubt the curious ones
wondered what had happened in the life of this
seemingly prosperous young man, obviously indifferent to physical appearance, to cause him to
join them.

John paid no attention to the passengers,
but hurried through the room and came to a halt
before a ticket window behind which a young
woman stood.

7

"Ticket, please," John ordered.

"Where to?" inquired the young woman pleasantly. If his disheveled appearance gave rise to any curiosity within her she did not show it.

"There's a bus loading at gate number 1," John answered, nodding in that direction. "Where is it goin'?"

"To Little Rock. Arrives tomorrow at 3 P.M."

"That will be okay. Make it Little Rock," he directed, reaching for his billfold.

"That will be $15.40," the ticket seller said as she placed the ticket in the stamping machine and pulled the lever noisily.

John tossed her a twenty-dollar bill, picked up the ticket where she had pushed it through to him, and grabbing up his bags, hurried toward the bus without waiting for his change.

The girl at the window reached mechanically for the bill as she opened the cash drawer. When she noticed her customer hastily departing she stared in his direction and opened her mouth as though to call to him, but evidently changed her mind and turned instead to speak into her microphone, at the same time extracting four one dollar bills and sixty cents change from the cash drawer, which she slipped into her skirt pocket as she reported to the driver of the bus.

"Hold it, Ted. Passenger to Little Rock."

She turned from her mike with a smile of satisfaction on her face as John surrendered his ticket and bags to the driver and entered the bus.

The bus was crowded and John found the only empty seat near the rear. He adjusted the seat to a half-reclining position, then lying back, pulled his hat down over his eyes and tried to relax. The vibration of the vehicle in motion, coupled with utter exhaustion, played its part and he was soon fast asleep.

It was then eleven P.M. and John slept restlessly through the night. When the morning sun shone brightly into the moving bus, he was fully aroused; although he dreaded facing life for even a day, he sat up to stretch his cramped muscles. Casting a glance out the window he noticed that the landscape was green and spring seemed much further advanced then it was in the northern part of Missouri where he had come from. The highway twisted and turned, following the path of least resistance through the rocky hills. Every high point gave a view of rugged beauty.

The driver pulled the bus into a small town, stopped before an unimpressive building labelled both "Cafe" and "Bus Depot" across its front windows, and announced a twenty minute stop for breakfast.

John was in no mood for eating, but was glad for the opportunity to get some exercise and fresh air. He filed out with the other passengers. When he entered the cafe, the odor of hot coffee caused him to decide upon a cup, soon followed by a second.

The fresh air seemed better to him than the stuffy bus and he was the last passenger to return. He resumed his seat near the window and continued to stare sulkily out of it mile after weary mile.

Near noon a tall, gaunt, unshaven man boarded the bus. He was dressed in freshly laundered, practical khaki-colored cotton twill pants and shirt, over which he wore a plain, dark suit coat. His gray felt hat was battered and ill-shaped, as though it had not received any care. The man looked quizzically about the bus and appeared to be unfamiliar with the art of traveling. Still, his mannerism, though somewhat awkward, was one of quiet dignity as he went about the business of finding an empty seat on the bus loaded almost to capacity.

The stranger's eyes came to rest on the empty seat beside John. He inquired matter-of-factly, "Anybody a settin' here?"

"No there isn't," John replied, as the hillman fitted his long frame into the seat beside him.

"Right purty day," the man stated as an opener for conversation, his friendliness asserting itself. To one born and bred in the hills it would seem "plumb unnatural" to ride along sitting in the same seat with another man and not show an interest in him.

"Yes, it is," John admitted readily, but added nothing to hold up his end of the conversation.

"You goin' fur?" the other questioned, undaunted by John's reticence.

"Little Rock," was the noncommittal response.

"Live there?"

"No," John replied, "I guess I don't live any place."

The hillman turned and looked at him searchingly. John didn't look like the kind of person who would have no home, although he did appear to be terribly unhappy. *There must be something wrong here,* he thought. Thereupon he set about finding out what it was.

"I knowed a feller what lived in Little Rock once. Right smart-sized place I guess," he eyed his companion furtively. When John made no reply, he continued, "Never been there myself. Think I'll go someday. Just to sorta look around a little bit."

John still was unresponsive, but his seat mate felt he had offered enough introductory remarks to entitle him to ask another question, so he inquired, "You been there before?"

"No," John answered, and, seeing that his companion was determined to talk, he decided he had just as well be friendly. Besides, he might learn something about the country through which they were passing from this man who was evidently a native. "No," he continued "I'm going there for the first time."

"Must be goin' to visit," his companion assumed. "Kinfolks, I reckon."

"No, not visit," John answered. "As a matter

of fact, I don't know what I'll do when I get there. Turn around and come back maybe." He spoke as much to himself as to his companion.

The man beside him began to feel defeated. He was sure his fellow traveler was having trouble and there just might be some way he could help, if he only knew where the difficulty lay. But then one never could tell.

"Where you figgerin' to go back to?"

John laughed. "That's a good question," he said, "I've got no place to go and nothing to do when I get there." And then he added in a bitter tone, "And I don't care."

This was the opening the hillman awaited and he lost no time in seizing the opportunity.

"Feller," he drawled, "I ain't aimin' to pry into another man's business, but when a body feels that way he's either lost his money or some woman's done him wrong."

If John had been thinking, he would have wondered about the ability of this unlearned hillman to analyze character. But his brain was so benumbed with the things that had happened to him that he was oblivious to almost everything except his own misery.

"I haven't lost any money," he responded. The hillman knew it was a woman, and seemed satisfied to let the matter rest.

Neither man spoke for a quarter of an hour. The man from the hills seemed occupied with his own thoughts and John continued to gaze through the window.

Finally John turned to the native and said, "This country is beautiful, but what do the people do for a living? Certainly they can't raise much cultivating those steep, rocky hills."

"Farmin' ain't so bad, pardner. Them rocky hills raises right smart. Kinda' tough a workin' though—lots o' rocks, stumps too, and when it's cleared, sprouts are bad. Persimmons are the worst. Seems like the only way to get rid of them is to dig and leave them. But them little fields raises right smart if a feller tends them good," the hillman replied.

"What crops do you raise?" John asked.

"Oh, most anything a feller plants. Most folks has a patch of wheat and corn for bread. Don't need much grain for fattenin'; most hogs they runs out on the range and fattens theirselves on acorns. Lots of wild berries, plums, apples and such does awful well. Last few years folks been araisin' termaters and strawberries since cannin' factories got so common. Them crops fetch right smart money. Most folks got a few cows—grass is good and it don't take much feedin' winters."

"What does this land sell for?" John interrupted.

"Some of it a feller can buy for the taxes, best of it 'bout twenty dollars an acre. Course, that's broke land, fenced, with house, barn and other buildings. Now me, I've got a quarter section, right snug cabin, log barn, hen house and spring house. I reckon it would fetch me ten dollars an acre."

"Do you have a family?" John continued questioning.

"Shore does — they's fourteen of us. Me and the woman has just a dozen young 'uns," the hillman said proudly.

"You have lots of help then," John said.

"They's eight of them big enough to work. All of us a'workin' to once can put out a patch of taters, corn or termaters in a hurry — don't take long to hoe them either," the man said as the bus swung into a little village filling station and restaurant.

"This is Hartstown, Missouri. We have a twenty minute stop for lunch here," the driver announced.

John and his loquacious seat mate made their way to the dining room. The neatly kept room was filled with small tables and a long food counter behind which stood the waitress, smiling and helpful.

John realized he was hungry and ordered a sandwich of country-cured ham.

"I reckon I'll be eatin' ham too," the hillman directed.

"What to drink?" the waitress asked.

"Coffee for me," John said.

"Me too," joined in the other.

"I have heard they make lots of moonshine whiskey in these mountains."

"Well, yes — not lots — but some. Most folks hereabouts don't have much to do with corn liquor. Some folks says they drink it to drown their troubles, but I reckon it only makes 'em worse."

"Then not many of these folks get tight?" John suggested.

"Tight — you mean drunk?" the hillman asked.

"Well, yes — tight they call it farther north, where I come from," John informed his companion.

"Yes, I've heard drunk folks called tight, but someway it just don't make sense, for they's loose instead of tight — loose talkin', loose actin' and right loose about bein' decent. Yes, I reckon loose would be right," the hillman philosophized.

"You're so right," John laughed. Then he asked, "Do you live around here?"

"Next town; it's about ten miles yet. This here's Hartstown. It's the county seat. Sixteen miles east of here is Wooded Lake. 'Lectric Company built a big dam across Spring River, flooded the whole valley, but it's purty down there. There's a little town between here and there, Clear Springs. It's on the river up above the lake. If I was you and wasn't right sure where I was goin' like you said, I'd go to Clear Springs. That'd be an awful good place to go to rest and get well and find out where you want to go. Good fishing there, too. Fishing's awful good medicine for any feller that's not sure of himself."

"Sounds like good advice," John answered with a slight smile, as they drained their coffee cups.

When they were again settled on the bus and on their way, John reached into his pocket and extracted a card with his name on it which he intended to hand to his new acquaintance. Then he abandoned the plan and withdrew his hand empty. Instead, he turned to the man beside him and said, "Someday I'd like to knock on your front door and hear more about this beautiful country. I'd better ask your name so I'll know how to find your place."

"My name's Henry. Henry Forbes. Hank, they call me. And stranger, you'd sure be welcome."

The bus was slowing down for the next stop and John's companion arose and extended his hand. "Good-by," he said, "and don't forget what I been telling you about what a little fishing can do for a feller that's feeling kinda low."

"Good-by," John said, shaking his hand. "Thank you, I'll not forget."

chapter 2

JOHN GAVE LITTLE THOUGHT to his departed companion after he left the bus, but lapsed into his mood of dark despair and gloom. When they finally pulled into the bus depot at Little Rock, he took his place in line with the other passengers, claimed his baggage, tipped the bus boy generously and entered the station. The time had come when he must choose a course of action. He could take another bus for a still more distant point, where he didn't care, or he could select a hotel and remain here in Little Rock for a few days. Almost mechanically he wandered over to the lunch counter where he ordered coffee. Brooding while he drank the beverage, strong and black, he realized that he was tired. He decided the best thing to do was to spend the next few days in Little Rock.

Having made up his mind, he paid for his coffee, picked up his bags and stepped out to hail a taxi. He instructed the driver to take him to a good hotel, explaining that he was a stranger in town and knew nothing of the accommodations available.

When he reached his room, John dismissed the bell boy with another generous tip and told him he desired no other service. When the boy had departed and the door was securely latched, he threw himself across the bed, weary to the point of exhaustion.

Sleep and relaxation did not come to him at once, however. His mind was in too great a turmoil for that, but John knew that he was going to have to get hold of himself, that no matter what happens to one, life must go on and that life must be useful, productive and worthwhile.

He lay stretched out on the bed with his right arm bent at the elbow and stretched across his eyes to shut out the light. He tried as he had a thousand times before to review the sequence of the events that had shaken his life apart since his return from the war only a week before.

John Malcom Smith hadn't wanted to go to war. He was in reality a conscientious objector, but he could scarcely bring himself to lay claim to the conviction as a reason why he should be excused from duty. He was fully as patriotic as any man being drafted into service, but he knew in his soul he could never go out and kill human beings without being tormented by his conscience. His spiritual convictions had been largely influenced by training from parents devout in the faith of the Quaker Church. To escape the ignominious stamp of being unpatriotic and at the same time to satisfy the demands made by his conscience, John listed a preference for the Air Corps when he was inducted. He hoped that because of his educational background he might be chosen to train as a navigator rather than to bear arms. Since not many inductees were seeking this extremely difficult and dangerous type of service, (neither were there many suited for it) John's request was granted and his arduous training began.

As was the case with many others, John had to leave a wife—Katherine. He was extremely reluctant, naturally, to leave her. They had married a year before he finished law school though he had felt then that it was a mistake not to wait until he was through school and had established a practice. But Katherine, a highly intelligent girl but rather spoiled and high strung, had insisted upon their being married. Her father, Judge Dalton, concurred in the idea. He also was a lawyer and for many years had been judge of Circuit Court. He knew that his daughter was impetuous and inclined to be a little wild. He felt that if she married a sober man like John Malcom Smith she would soon settle down.

Judge Dalton liked John, who was an earnest, sincere young man of high intelligence with every prospect of going far in his chosen profession. The judge knew, however, that although John came from a fine family, they were poor and it was somewhat of a struggle for them to finance John's education. As a matter of fact, John was working at various jobs to help pay expenses. Judge Dalton promised that if John and Katherine were married he would continue to give Katherine her generous allowance until John had finished school. Although

John would rather have married later when he could assume full responsibility for the support of his wife, he permitted himself to be persuaded, because of his great love for Katherine.

At first, things went well. They were deeply in love with each other and Kathy, as John called his new bride, seemed quite happy and content to keep house for the two of them in their small apartment. She took great interest in his studies and their evenings were spent mostly in preparing his assignments.

After John's graduation, Katherine's father offered them a fine big house which he owned. John objected so strenuously that the judge contented himself with allowing the young married couple to live in the house rent free for five years, with an option to buy if they chose to do so. John had a serious talk with the judge, explaining that he and Katherine preferred to work out their problems for themselves, financial and otherwise, without any help from others. The old man respected their wishes, never again offering them such assistance.

Nor had they needed it. When John graduated he went in with a small though well-known law firm. Later he struck out on his own. He held to his firm belief in honesty and integrity. Although his profits had not been staggering, he did well and was able to buy Katherine almost anything she wanted. He had long since paid her father for the big house, had money in the bank along with some good securities. Better than that, he was steadily building up an enviable practice.

So things had been when he left for the war. Through all the long weary months of waiting, his constant prayer was to be permitted to return to Kathy.

His part in the war had been hard. He had successfully completed forty-six bombing missions with only four more to go before he could go home. Some of them had been uneventful. Others were fraught with danger. He had seen much blood shed by dozens of his comrades. It was all horrible and seemed terribly futile. With so much hatred and chaos in the world John found it difficult at times to keep his faith in God intact. Only by looking ahead with hope in his heart and a prayer on his lips could he carry on from day to day.

Then, on his forty-seventh flight into the combat zone, his plane was shot down. Rather, it was blasted apart in the air. John was sure that all the crew were dead or mortally wounded before the last terrific explosion occurred. He, himself, had a painful bullet wound in his shoulder which bled profusely. When the pilot slumped over in his seat during the merciless firing from the enemy plane, John took over the controls, hoping to bring the great machine to the earth. Then suddenly the whole tail assembly and mid-section of the ship burst into flame. John, knowing that no power on earth could save the plane nor the men aboard, dead or living, quickly took advantage of his opportunity to escape sure death and jumped from the aerial furnace. He never did remember what happened after that.

Many days later he regained consciousness to discover that he was being cared for by a family in the French underground. He had fallen in a field of boulders near a tiny stream, where he had lain for some time before being rescued. A French girl, Nanette, who had seen his parachute and would not rest until she found him, finally located him. He was suffering not only from the wound in his shoulder but also a badly crushed ankle broken when he landed between two huge rocks that formed the entrance to a large cave.

Nanette lived nearby with her mother and father. Their home was really underground, for they had dug out a clearing far back under a bluff. The entrance was obscured by enormous rocks and a thick growth of small trees and shrubs. When the girl found John she loosened his clothing, removed his boots and ran back to the house for a pail of water. She gave him a drink and applied cold compresses to his injured ankle and shoulder. When it grew dark she brought her father and mother and they carried him to their home.

Finally after long dreary months of hiding and waiting—months that stretched into the second year—while he grew intermittently impatient and depressed because he could get no word from Kathy, or to her, because of the danger of discovery

—the day of liberation came and he entered a base hospital in England for physical examination. After that he was shipped home to be discharged as no longer physically fit for military service. Moved from one medical department to another so rapidly that he didn't have an opportunity to cable or telephone Kathy, John forgot to be concerned because he was no longer the perfect physical specimen who had entered the service of his country many months before. Plenty of time for that later . . . Now his mind was all on Kathy and he chafed at every bit of red tape and regulation which delayed him.

In the first moment of freedom after disembarking at New York he placed a call to Kathy. His heart pounded so hard in his throat that he was afraid he couldn't hear when she answered. He tried to imagine what she would say to him while he waited impatiently for the call to be completed. Perhaps he shouldn't have called. She hadn't heard from him all these months. No doubt she would get quite a shock when she heard his voice. He had no more time for thinking for the operator was telling him that his party was on the line and the next instant he heard Katherine's voice.

chapter 3

"KATHY," JOHN SHOUTED excitedly into the phone. "Kathy, darling. This is John. I'm in New York."

"No! No!" and a piercing scream came over the wire to him followed by a dreadful silence. John was frantic. He had been right. The shock was too much for her and she had been overcome. What was he to do? He rattled the receiver furiously to get the operator back on the line. The operator responded in a few moments to say that the number could not be reached as the receiver was off the hook.

John condemned himself for having been such a fool. Why hadn't he forseen such an event?

Poor Kathy, he thought, *what a strain she has been under. Why, she didn't even know if I was dead or alive.*

John left the telephone booth to pace up and down. Then he returned and placed a call to Judge Dalton. If he had had any sense, he thought bitterly, that is what he would have done in the first place.

Thirty minutes elapsed before John had Judge Dalton on the wire. He told him that Katherine was indeed overcome by his sudden return and was under sedatives. He advised John that although her condition was serious it was not necessarily critical. The Judge spoke gravely and John himself was in a daze. He upbraided himself severely. How could he have been so inconsiderate? He told his father-in-law that he would be there just as soon as he possibly could make it.

He returned to his base where he explained the situation to the authorities and was granted an emergency leave. Taking a taxi to the airport and finding no plane due to leave for several hours, he chartered a private plane and was in the air in a few minutes. In Chicago John wired Judge Dalton when to meet him at the airport. John tried his best to think rationally, but his brain kept pounding in his head. He could never forgive himself for what he had done to Kathy, but he knew everything would be all right as soon as he could reach her. He couldn't forget the strained voice with which Judge Dalton spoke to him. Surely if Katherine were all right her father would not have appeared so worried.

The long anxious flight ended and they landed at the once familiar airport just at the break of day. John sighted Judge Dalton as he came through the gate to meet him. The judge's face was pale and he looked worn and haggard. *How much he has aged,* John thought as he advanced toward him. From the look on the judge's face Kathy must be very ill.

They met, each clasping the extended hand of the other.

"How is she?" John asked. His face, too, was drawn and pale.

The judge lifted his face and looked squarely at his son-in-law. John was shocked at what he saw in the aging man's face. Not fear, not grief, but dark despair and defeat. "Better," he said and dropped his eyes.

"Thank God!" said John. "I came as quickly as I could."

John wasn't thinking or he would have noticed that the judge was slow and hesitant about going to Katherine. Once in the car and driving away the younger man felt that at last he could relax. Only a few minutes and everything would be all right.

Neither of the men said anything until Mr. Dalton turned into the driveway to his home. Then John turned to inquire, "Is Kathy here? I thought—"

Before he had finished his father-in-law had stopped the car under the portico at the side of his great house. Turning to John, he said with feeling, "My boy, come in."

They entered the house and the judge began to talk in a slow, dull, tired voice, "Son," he said, "you must get hold of yourself for I have the worst possible kind of news for you."

"Oh, please, Mr. Dalton," John exploded, "tell me. What has happened to Kathy?" He was almost shouting and perspiration stood out on his forehead while his hands felt cold and clammy.

The old judge raised his eyes to look at John and stood there as one paralyzed. Never in his life afterwards was John Smith able to forget the awful agony of soul that was registered in his father-in-law's countenance. He opened his mouth two times as if to speak and then sensing John's impatience and bewilderment the old gentleman collapsed into a nearby chair and buried his face in his hands. He gave way to uncontrollable sobs. John thought he was going to go mad.

The older man mumbled over and over, "I can't say it! It's too awful for words."

John raised the judge to his feet and shook him. "Calm yourself, sir," he said, making his own manner as steady as possible. "You are not being fair. I must know about Kathy." John felt by now that he was surely prepared for anything and no matter what had happened to his Kathy he would stand by her and care for her. He visualized her as being crippled perhaps. Or maybe blindness had come upon her. Or she might be afflicted with some dreadful disease. Whatever it was he and Kathy could be together and everything would be all right.

Finally Mr. Dalton had regained his self-control and he said in a voice weary with defeat, "John, she is married."

"Married?" John wanted to laugh. "Of course she is married. She's married to me," he shouted. He looked at his father-in-law. The poor old fellow. He must be unbalanced. The strain of the long years of war no doubt had been too much for him. After all Kathy had three brothers that had been inducted and John didn't know but that they had been lost.

But the news bearer didn't seem the least bit relieved. In fact greater tragedy than ever showed in his face if that was possible.

"John," he said severely, "you don't understand. Kathy thought you were dead and she has remarried."

"Married! Dead!" John repeated incredulously, feeling as if the earth had rocked beneath him. "Why that's impossible. I'm not dead. And she's married to me. Do you hear, sir? Kathy's married to me." He was wildly shouting again.

The judge was more in command of the situation now than his son-in-law. "Sit down, John," he ordered sternly. "This is a terrible situation, but we have to face it and see what can be done."

John sank weakly into a chair as he began to grasp the dreadful truth.

Slowly the judge began to talk. "Son, two years ago this month Katherine received a message from the War Department that you were missing in action. She was so upset that we had all we could do to keep her steady and she spent endless hours day and night, urging various agencies to trace all sorts of clues that might lead to some sort of news of you. She even hired private detectives to help in the search, but all to no avail. I'm sure no stone was left unturned, but she never gave up until a message finally came from the War Department that you had been declared officially dead. By that time we had gotten the details of what had happened to you and since your plane was totally demolished and no member of the crew was ever heard from again you were all assumed to be lost.

"That was eighteen months ago. We all urged Katherine to become active in war work to get her mind off her loss. She became a hostess at the U.S.O. unit here and I'll have to admit there were times when she sort of went the limit. She was always a little unstable as you well know, but I didn't know what to do. I was nearly worried to death about her brothers. They were all three in the combat zone. Well, the outcome of it all was that Katherine fell head over heels in love with Neil Hamilton and they were married six months ago."

"Neil Hamilton!" John bellowed as he pounded his clenched fists on the arms of his chair. "What was he doing here? Why wasn't he in the war?"

John knew Neil Hamilton well. His father was a wealthy manufacturer and had a huge home there in the small town where John had lived. Neil was supposed to be a junior partner in his father's business, but most of his time was spent in driving sporty convertibles from one point of pleasure to another.

"Well," the judge said, "you know how those things are. He just never seemed to be called."

"Yes, how well I know," John exploded savagely. "I come home and find the yellow sniveling cur has stolen an honest man's wife."

"Not stolen, John," Mr. Dalton soothed. "You will have to grant that both he and Kathy, no matter how tragic their marriage has turned out to be, acted in good faith. They thought you were dead."

"Take me to Kathy," John ordered, "I'll have this marriage annulled." But even as he spoke, John knew such an action would not right the wrong that had been done.

"The situation is not as simple as all that," Mr. Dalton advised. "And you can't see Kathy now."

But John interrupted, "Why can't I see her?"

"Because," explained her father, "the doctor says she must be kept very quiet. You see, son, she is expecting a baby and the shock of having you return under such circumstances is causing a great deal of trouble."

He walked over and laid his hand on John's shoulder, "John," he said, "pull yourself together. You, Katherine and Hamilton will have to reach an agreement, but at the moment it will be better for you to go away for a while."

"Yes, I'll go away," John said bitterly. At last someone was talking sense. He wanted to get away fast and he wanted to go far.

chapter 4

JOHN DIDN'T KNOW how long he had lain upon the bed in the hotel room in Little Rock. It was however, long enough for his tired body to become rested while his mind continued to review over and over the succession of events that had laid him low.

Now he became restless and rose from the bed, smoothed his hair from force of habit and went down to the dining room for a cup of coffee. He sat dejectedly at a counter and from his seat he could see men and women going in and out of the cocktail lounge.

"Would it help to get drunk?" John wondered. He had never been drunk. In fact he had never tasted liquor. His parents had been adamant in their opposition to intoxicating liquors and John had grown up to abhor all liquors and the habit of drinking. Now he knew he would never resort to drinking even when nothing appealed to him so much as absolute oblivion. He had seen many a soldier get drunk to help him forget, but it always turned out to be only an unsuccessful means of dealing with a problem, for the drunk must wake up sooner or later only to find the problem still there and his ability to cope with it greatly diminished.

John drained his coffee cup and walked aimlessly out of the hotel into the street. He scanned the scene to the left and then to the right and began walking. Block after block fell behind him until he reached the outskirts of the city and then, because there seemed to be no place else to go, he turned and retraced his steps. Tomorrow he would return to his base in New York. He would have to go through the tedious business of separating from the army. After that he would decide on something. Perhaps he would stay in New York. With the war still going on it would be relatively easy to get established in the law business almost anywhere. It wouldn't be necessary for him to have to return home. Judge Dalton would take care of his affairs there. John was sure that he never wanted to see any of his former friends again. He was glad his parents were no longer living.

By the time John had returned to his hotel it was far past midnight. He had stopped to eat at a small cafe on the way and found himself to be ravenously hungry. When he got into bed he fell into a deep sleep from which he did not awaken until nearly noon.

Upon arising he made plans to return to New York and soon after lunch was on his way. Being mustered out consumed several days. Then John Malcom Smith was a free man.

Free indeed! John thought bitterly. Free to create a life without Kathy, for by now he knew he could never claim Katherine as his own. He could not do it because she was to have a child. He could not ever again believe in Kathy who had been so quickly reconciled after he had been declared dead. *And so easily reconciled too,* John thought, for no two men could possibly be more unlike than Neil Hamilton and himself. John was more enraged now against Katherine than against Hamilton for whom he had never held anything but contempt. It seemed outrageous that any intelligent woman could be attracted to such a weak, unscrupulous character.

John was beginning to realize now, however, as he reviewed his life with Katherine, that much of the time they had had little in common. Katherine had been fun-loving and socially ambitious. She was often indiscreet and seemed to care little for what anyone thought of her moral conduct, while she guarded anxiously her position of social leadership. The most important factors in her life were to be able to give the biggest parties, wear the nicest clothes, and drive the classiest cars. John had pretended to be interested in these social affairs when actually he was not only bored but felt downright imposed upon by such a waste of time, energy and money.

Early in their marriage John had put his foot down about their drinking at parties. He was shocked when he discovered that champagne was being served at their wedding reception and he gave his bride to understand then that never would any intoxicants be served in their home and neither would they drink liquor at social functions. Many times she had argued the point with him and told him there was no harm in social drinking and that he was just old fashioned. But John remained firm in his conviction that indulging in the drinking of alcoholic beverages was not only foolish but also unbecoming a Christian. He pointed out to Kathy that certainly drinking was wrong for church members and specifically to him because he was the teacher of a class of junior boys.

"They would never know whether you drank or not," she would argue.

"But I would know," John would reply, "and I couldn't face those boys nor God unless I was honest with them and with myself."

"Well, why do you have to teach a Sunday school class?" Kathy would inquire. "You spend such a lot of time studying for it. When the other fellows are out on Saturday afternoons playing golf you are sitting in that stuffy old den preparing a Sunday school lesson."

John tried always to be patient with Kathy. He loved her a great deal and felt sure she didn't mean the things she said. She was so young and pretty and loved so much to be admired that it was hard for her to cling to precepts that kept her from being one of the crowd.

"Kathy," he would say gently, "when I decided to become a Christian I made up my mind that I was going to be the very best sort that it was possible for me to be.

"I know I fall far short of what I should do, but there is one thing you must never ask of me and that is to forsake my faith. So long as I live I shall be doing what I can for the cause of Christ." And then he would remind her. "You knew those were my convictions when you married me."

Then Kathy would apologize and kissing him would say, "I'm sorry, darling. I really am awfully proud of you. Only I don't see why you had to pick such a strict church to belong to. You know there are churches that don't preach so much against drinking and having a good time."

Then John would say severely, "Katherine Smith, there isn't a Christian church in existence that doesn't condemn the evil of drinking and the social looseness that goes with it. It is true that there are many preachers who either condone or ignore many social evils, but certainly they do not speak for the churches."

Usually the discussion would terminate there, but from time to time it would rise between them again and John would feel much more distressed than Kathy ever seemed to realize.

It was about the only point of dissension between them and it seemed to John that the arguments became more heated after Kathy left the small community church where he had long been a member and became the organist at a large, fashionable church downtown.

It wasn't that Kathy was opposed to attend-

ing church. Her father had taken her to Sunday
school as a child and she had joined the church
when only ten years old. Nearly all of the children
of her social set became members of the church by
arrangement with their pastor. The parents seemed
to think it was a very proper thing for a child
to do, but little importance as to the child becoming Christ-like was attached to it. Parents
taught their children that the best people belong to
the church and there were many advantages to it
if it was not carried too far.

Many of the children when they reached the
age of adolescence dropped the habit of attending
church, but not Katherine Dalton. She had great
ability for leadership and no activity provided the
field for it as did the church. Her special talent was
music and dramatic art, so she became a youth-
ful member of the choir, dressing always for church
attendance with delicate taste and girlish simplicity.
Her happy reward was the wonderful esteem in
which she was held by members of the congregation
and the pastor.

Judge Dalton had insisted upon his daughter
attending Sunday school in her childhood because
he was very anxious that she be highly developed
intellectually. He knew of no better way of intro-
ducing her to the best in history and literature than
a study of the Bible. He also enjoyed immensely
the privileges of teaching a class of young married
people. Judge Dalton considered himself something
of a scholar and he cherished the opportunity of

expounding his personal observations of the Biblical account, scoffing at those stories that to him seemed unreasonable and delineating at great length on the particular ones that appealed to his common sense as being within the range of plausibility. Because he dared to disagree with ideas that were often unquestionably accepted by many, and also because he had the ability to present his arguments so brilliantly, the young folk who were his pupils acclaimed him as a deep thinker. When the judge entered politics he discovered that his years of service in the church had rewarded him with many votes.

It had never been the judge's habit to attend the worship service regularly, however. Usually when a new pastor came to serve the church he would go for a few Sundays but the messages were so often sort of disturbing to a man's peace of mind that he would stay away rationalizing that the ministry needed a good dose of modernizing. Could not a preacher ever get it into his head that a man liked to go to church to worship and relax and not to have his mind disturbed about the condition of his soul? But after Katherine began singing in the choir her father became a regular attendant at morning worship and sat near the front of the sanctuary, beaming proudly upon his daughter, chief among her admirers. He, too, liked the pastor whose sermons were delightful discourses on the various psychological aspects of religion that were becoming so popular both from the pulpit and the press. John had heard the man a few times and always came away feeling a bit bewildered. Not that anyone could find anything in the sermon with which to disagree, but there always seemed so little for one to carry away with him. John could never understand why a man would utilize forty-five minutes to bring a message that could easily be cut down to ten minutes without leaving out a single idea.

But then, John's religious training had been different. He had been taught from infancy that the most important thing in one's life was his relationship to God. Church attendance was as much a part of his pattern of living as eating his meals or getting up in the morning. He had been guided in reading Bible stories to learn the great lessons of faith and courage and salvation through Jesus Christ. His parents had taught well, both by living examples and by precept. John had accepted Christ with a wholehearted desire to be of service to God and his fellowman.

John was again walking aimlessly in a strange town trying to decide what to do while his thoughts filled his mind and as he thought it all over he was more or less of the opinion that he would have lost Katherine sooner or later anyway.

After several hours, John stopped short, *Where am I?* he wondered. He had walked for many blocks. Suddenly, discovering that he was extremely tired, he flung himself on a nearby park bench.

I don't know where I am and I don't know where I'm going, he mused.

Then he remembered he had said something of that sort to a kindly native on the bus who had answered, "Reckon if a feller went out to Clear Springs 'mongst them folks and jest set a spell or fished right smart, he'd soon be right sure where he was goin'."

John pondered the statement seriously. He was strongly tempted to go. It sounded ridiculous to think that a man would be influenced to visit a place just because he had heard a perfect stranger extol its virtues. But as a matter of fact he had read a great deal about the Ozarks and had often thought how much he would like to visit the region. Even in his state of agitation while riding through on the bus just a few days before, he had been thrilled with the wonderful scenery and the peaceful quietude.

"It may be just the thing I need," John concluded rising from the bench. "I'll go there. If I have to spend some time finding out what to do next, I'd just as well do some of it fishing."

chapter 5

HAVING MADE UP HIS MIND to return to the Ozark country, John lost no time in getting started in that direction. He was not a man who acted on impulse, but neither did he deliberate long in making decisions. Now he was anxious to get out of New York. He had to choose between the discomfort of a bus or the discomfort of an overcrowded train, since one needed priority for plane travel. He decided upon the train because he believed it to be the least tiresome and perhaps less time-consuming.

He bought a ticket to Springfield, Missouri and arrived some twenty-six hours later. Then he took a bus to Hartstown, not knowing how he would proceed from there, but at least he would be down in the heart of the Ozarks and not far from Clear Springs. He had noticed when he had gone through that country to Little Rock that there were accommodations for tourists at most of the towns.

When he arrived at Hartstown he found that although it was a county seat, there was only a small hotel. Still, the room the proprietor showed him was clean and spacious enough to be comfortable. He paid for one night's lodging.

The next day he inquired of the hotel proprietor about good places to fish and in the conversation mentioned Clear Springs.

"Clear Springs is not really a town," the hotel keeper said. "There's only a post office and a few houses there. But it is on Spring River where fishing is very good. The country is rugged, but there are a lot of fine folk that live there."

"Is Spring River a mountain stream?" John inquired.

"It sure is. Fed from springs. That's where it got its name. Rock bottom and the water is clear and sparkling. I tell you there just isn't a better place to fish. I go there every time I can get away. Of course, it's awfully quiet there so if you're looking for solid comfort and folks around it wouldn't suit you." The man spoke as though he feared John would turn out to be the kind that would not appreciate the place and he seemed disappointed.

"What kind of fish?" John asked. "Trout?"

"There sure is!" the proprietor answered, beaming with enthusiasm.

"That's good enough for me," John replied and the man behind the desk seemed altogether happy. "Is there a place where I could stay down there? Maybe I could set up a tent."

"There are some cabins. Belong to John Gurney. Rents them for a dollar a night. Now, there has been a lot of development over at Lake City. It's a new town where the dam is built. It's a resort town and there is lots of excitement and people over there. You'd be more comfortable there perhaps," the hotel man offered gingerly.

"I don't care about the comfort and I certainly don't care about the people."

John inquired how he could get to Clear Springs and was told by the proprietor that he could go on the mail truck that left from the local post office daily at 1:30 P.M.

The emotionally disturbed man was in no mood for the two and a half hour wait imposed upon him until the mail truck arrived to take him to Clear Springs, but since he had no alternative, he sat brooding in the sunshine, forgetting altogether to eat his noon meal.

When 1:30 finally rolled around John was restlessly pacing back and forth in front of the post office. As the driver of the half-ton truck drove up, ready for the daily trip, he looked sharply at John's fashionably cut clothes and grinned ruefully.

"Do you want a ride to Clear Springs?" he inquired.

John replied that he did and asked if there was room for him.

"Not in the cab, there ain't," the driver returned apologetically. "I've already got two passengers in the cab. Picked 'em up at the hardware store. The first ones to ask get to ride in the front."

"I understand," John answered. "I'd like to get to Clear Springs today. May I ride in the back?"

"You sure can, but it's kinda bumpy back there."

"I won't mind," John answered as he threw his luggage into the bed of the truck. Climbing aboard he seated himself on an overturned wooden box and the driver started the bumpy ride over the rough roads to Clear Springs.

John gave little heed to the jostling and lurching of the truck as it rattled along its way. Actually, the physical discomfort of the ride was a welcome contrast to the hurt in his soul. Each painful bump was easier to bear than the stab that penetrated his brain with every thought of the things that had happened to him.

Up hill and down over the rocky, rough road the driver persisted until they rounded a curve and came suddenly upon a level clearing dotted with two or three dwelling places and a long one-story frame store building badly in need of paint.

A loading platform stretched across the front of the building. As the truck came to a full stop, John rose. His eyes rested upon a long weather beaten board extending from one edge of the roof to the other. On it, in faded black paint, he read:

CLEAR SPRINGS
POST OFFICE AND GENERAL STORE
DAVE GURNEY, PROPRIETOR

The owner had put it there many years ago, not so much to inform an inquiring public, as to follow the dictum of arbitrary regulations.

John alighted from the truck, claimed his belongings and entered the store.

A dozen or more people sat around on nail kegs, low hickory bottom chairs or along the edge of the counters, but there seemed to be no proprietor. As the stranger came in, each person present eyed him furtively. Conversation ended abruptly as though each participant suddenly found himself burdened with much upon which to meditate. Then John noticed a small box-like room in the corner of the store where he observed through a slated opening, a huge man, dressed in khaki colored covert shirt and gallused pants of the same material, sorting the mail that had just been delivered. Most of his patrons were out front in the store and had lined up expectantly before the window.

"Big Dave," as John was later to learn the owner of the store was called, stepped up to the window and boomed out names of the various patrons of the post office as he read from the letters, cards and occasional magazines he held in his hand.

"Barnes, Clayton, Pemberton, Hull," were a few of the names John heard called out and as each man's name was called he stepped up to the window, received his day's quota and perusing it carefully walked from the store. John noticed that many if not most of the envelopes bore evident marks of having been written by persons in the armed services. He reflected that even in this remote, isolated section of the world the great conflict had brought tears and anxiety and sacrifice.

Some of those who had come to await the arrival of the mail had not been called. They turned away with a sigh. The postmaster emerged from his retreat and spoke softly to those who had been disappointed. He was especially kind to one of the women. She was neatly dressed in a freshly laundered print dress. Her coal black hair was drawn to the back of her head and pinned low on her neck in a tight roll. She wore heavy, brown oxfords that were covered with dust, indicating that she had walked from her home to the post office.

"Too bad you didn't get a letter today, Mandy," he said, "but it will probably come tomorrow. George ain't a goin' to forget to write." His attempt to be cheerful was unsuccessful, however, The woman addressed as Mandy brushed a tear from her face.

"No, George won't forget," she replied. "He'll write whenever he can, but its been more than two months now." She picked up a small basket of groceries and walked listlessly from the store.

All the others had gone and Big Dave turned to the stranger, "Poor Mandy!" he lamented, shaking his grizzly head. "I shore wish she'd get a letter from George. I'm getting so I hate to see mail time come 'cause I hate so bad to tell her there ain't no letter. And I know she'll be here waitin'. She comes every day. Never misses and its more than a three mile walk."

John nodded and the store proprietor continued, "I'll sure be glad when this horrible war is over. Mandy never complains, but she lots of times says she can't understand what all the fightin's about."

"Neither can a lot of the rest of us," John broke in and Big Dave seemed to remember he had a customer.

"Oh, yes," he said, "What can I do for you, sir?"

"I have come here to do a little fishing," John explained, "and I wondered about a place to stay. Perhaps a cabin."

"Well, now, you've sure come to the right place," Big Dave continued. "Spring River is the best place to fish in this whole country. The water sparkles so pretty when it comes rippling down over the rocks. Makes the purtiest music a man ever heard. And not enough folks have come in from the outside to spoil things yet."

The man must be spokesman for the Clear Springs Chamber of Commerce, John thought ruefully, wondering when he was going to get a word in edgewise.

"I was wondering if I could get a cabin," he repeated.

"Well, now, I got some little cabins. My brother John takes care of 'em for me. But there's nary a one of 'em empty right now. Got 'em filled up with fellers like you wantin' to do some fishin'. But I reckon John can take care of you in his own house. He lives all by himself and has extra rooms. If you wouldn't mind staying in a house instead of a cabin."

John did mind. He much preferred a cabin where he could be by himself. But since he now was in Clear Springs, too late to turn back, he would have to find a place to stay.

"Where does your brother live?" he inquired.

"That's my house across the road," Dave Gurney explained. "And John's house is just a little step down the road. Built right on the river bank. He used to run the old mill."

"May I leave my things here while I go down and inquire about a room?" John asked politely.

"Sure. And John can come back with you and help you pack your stuff down there. By the way, my name's Gurney. Big Dave they call me. Don't reckon I know your name."

"Smith," John said, grasping Dave Gurney's extended hand in a mighty clasp. And then he added deliberately, "John Malcom Smith. I'd like for you to call me Mal. Short for Malcom you know. It was my mother's name before her marriage."

John had made up his mind that he was some how or other going to build a new life for himself and he believed that if he changed his name it would help to make him over into another person. In fact he was already different. The war was responsible for that. John hated cruelty and suffering and death and being mixed up in so much of it had destroyed much of his faith in God and man. If God was just and kind and loving, why did He permit such wanton destruction? If man was His noblest creation, why did he engage in the demoralizing and sinful business of destroying his fellowman? These questions were already troubling him before he had arrived home to find his lovely Kathy belonging to someone else and gone from him forever.

John decided he would not adopt an alias. It was not as though he were running away or in hiding. He was proud of the name Smith and proud of his family inheritance. He would not "sell his birthright." But he believed if he were to become Malcom Smith instead of John Smith he would more readily build himself into a personality who had no part in things that had ruined the old life.

"Smith's right common," Big Dave mused. "Mal Smith. I kinda like it. Easy to handle and right purty. Sounds like water surgin' among the rocks."

"Thank you, Mr. Gurney," John said. "Now if you'll excuse me, I'll go to see your brother about a place to sleep."

chapter 6

MAL SMITH, as he came to be called, encountered no difficulty in finding lodging with John Gurney the miller.

"Sure, I've got a loft room. Stairway's outside so it will be as private as you like. The bed is made up and the room is clean. Rosie, she's my girl that's married now, cleaned it up yesterday. She comes over and cleans up everything one day a week." John was talking all the way up the stairs with Mal following close behind.

The outside staircase, common in the Ozarks, was built to conserve space inside the house. The stair landing on the same level as the upstairs floor was about fourteen feet square. The door of the room was of oak and handmade. The room they entered, while small, was cheerful and comfortable. Bright rays of light and sunshine filtered into the room through windows on the south and west. There was also a window on the north side that admitted light and fresh air. The entire floor was covered with a hand woven rag carpet. Crisply starched and freshly hung curtains were at each window. A massive old-fashioned bed, a marble top table and a small chest of drawers made up the bedroom suite. The group would have commanded a small fortune in an antique shop. On the marble

49

top table rested a beautiful kerosene lamp with the globe and bowl hand painted in matching design. A straight chair and low rocker completed the room furniture.

"This will do nicely," Mal said reaching for his billfold. "How much is it?"

"Well, I never thought the day would come when I'd charge a feller for a place to sleep, but since the war everything has been so high. And I can't work much anymore," John Gurney faltered. "We charge a feller a dollar a night for the cabins, but I reckon this here room wouldn't be worth so much. About two and a half a week, I reckon."

"When will you have a cabin available?" John inquired.

"The fellers that are down there now, there's six of 'em, two in each cabin, will leave a week from today. If you want you can have a cabin then."

"Splendid. But this room looks very comfortable and I'm sure a dollar a night for it would be only reasonable."

"Nope," John demurred. "Jist give me two dollars and four bits. I don't feel very good about taking money like this no way. It's a pleasure to have you. Now I'll help you get your things."

"How about meals?" Mal wanted to know. "I presume there is someone in the community that would serve board."

"Sure is. Mrs. Morgan. About a mile down the trail. She's a widow. Married Squire Morgan up at Oak Ridge and then he up and died and she moved down there in the holler and begun feedin' folks that have been coming in here lately to fish and hunt. But you don't need to bother goin' down there tonight. I'll coddle up a little bite and you can eat supper with me."

"That's very kind of you," Mal replied. They were now on their way to Dave's store for Mal's things. "But I'm afraid I'd be imposing on you."

"Not at all," John assured him. "Be right proud to have you. I get kinda lonesome like sometimes."

While John prepared the evening meal, Mal established himself in the "loft" room. Then after eating a hearty supper of fried potatoes, ham, rich brown gravy, great hunks of corn bread and coffee, he took a stroll along the river before going to bed.

In no time at all he was sleeping and did not hear a sound until the light of day filled his room and awakened him. He arose, dressed quietly and crept softly down the stairs, trying carefully not to disturb his host. Standing on the stair landing Mal breathed deeply of the invigorating morning air. *What a country*, he thought as he stood enchanted by the rugged timbered hills. The hilltops and upper slopes were gleaming in the first rays of the rising sun. In the foreground the mist hung low like lace over Spring River. Looking at his watch he was surprised to learn it was only five o'clock.

Mal need not have been so cautious for John Gurney was sitting under a tree in the yard.

John greeted his guest and said he had been trying to keep "kinda quiet" so as not to awaken him.

"I reckoned you were pretty tired," he said. "Did you sleep all right?"

"I never slept better," Mal replied, "Didn't wake up all night. I don't know when I last slept like that."

"A man with a clear conscience can sleep in this mountain air," John said. "Now you go down to the spring and wash up a bit. You'll find a towel and a wash pan there. I'll fix some breakfast."

"But I'm going to Mrs. Morgan's for my meals," Mal objected.

"No need to go over there until after breakfast. I got the coffee makin' and it won't take long to fry some meat and eggs."

John disappeared into the kitchen and Mal followed the path to the spring which he found to be gurgling delightfully up out of the ground. All around was verdant beauty. The ground was sodden from the springs' overflow and beds of dark green vegetation grew in large patches. Mal was later to learn that the plant was water cress and was delicious in green salads. He plunged a gourd dipper that was hanging nearby into the water and drank of the sparkling cold liquid. *No wonder these people continue to believe in God,* he thought. *It's easy to see that God furnishes this spring of water in a miraculous way. But when all the water one needs is supplied by turning a metal faucet designed and installed by man himself, it sometimes becomes difficult to remember God's part in the scheme of things.*

After breakfast, Mal lost no time in taking the trail to the home of Mrs. Morgan to arrange for his meals. He didn't feel comfortable about accepting John Gurney's hospitality although he knew it was sincerely offered to him.

Mrs. Morgan's home was a long, old-fashioned two story house with a wide porch stretching all the way across the front. It was picturesquely set far back from the dusty road in a grove of large oak and hickory trees.

Mal strolled up the long flagstone walk and rapped on the front door. A young girl answered the knock.

"I understand the owner of this place serves meals," he stated politely. "I've come to make arrangements to secure my meal's here."

By this time Mrs. Morgan, a stout lady of short stature and pleasant face, had come to the door. The young girl went back into the house.

"Yes, sir, I serve meals," Mrs. Morgan declared in answer to Mal's query.

"Then may I eat my meals with you?" Mal asked. "I'm a stranger here. I'm staying with John Gurney and expect to do some fishing the next few days."

"Lots of folks are coming here to fish now

days," Mrs. Morgan interpolated. "But I thought John's cabins were all full. They's six men eatin' here and they said they were asleepin' in his cabins in pairs. He's only got three cabins."

Mal thought he detected a note of suspicion in Mrs. Morgan's questioning. He had heard many times of the native Ozarker's wariness in dealing with strangers.

"Mr. Gurney's cabins *are* all occupied," he explained, "but he was kind enough to allow me to stay in an upstairs room until he has a cabin vacant. He suggested that I could eat here with you."

"Sure you can," Mrs. Morgan replied genially. Mal couldn't be sure whether it was her suspicions or curiosity that had been allayed. "Come right in now and I'll fix you some breakfast." The housewife had pushed the screen door open and was waving her hand through the air to keep the flies from entering.

"Thank you," Mal hastened to say, "but I had breakfast with Mr. Gurney this morning. If it is agreeable I should—"

"Now if that ain't just like John Gurney. I never did see such a man for puttin' himself out to accommodate other folks." Mrs. Morgan broke in, closing the screen door with a little bang.

"He certainly is a very kind and hospitable person," Mal agreed, wondering when he would be released from this talkative woman's flow of gossip.

"At what hour do you serve lunch, Mrs. Morgan?" he inquired patiently.

"Lunch?" she began. "Oh, you mean dinner. Dinner's at twelve, supper at six and you can have breakfast any time you want it up to nine o'clock mornings."

"That will be fine and you may expect me to be back by noon," Mal said. "How about your rates? What do you charge?"

"I charge a dollar and a half a day, sir. I know it's kinda high and it wouldn't be so much if I could raise part of my stuff but it keeps me busy doing the cooking."

"It isn't too high, Mrs. Morgan. In fact, it is quite reasonable," Mal hastened to say, making a mental note that he probably had just made the understatement of the year, food prices being what they were. "Shall I pay you for a week's board in advance?"

"Well, I hate to ask it," Mrs. Morgan began and Mal hurriedly deposited ten dollars and fifty cents in her hand before she launched into an explanation. "I'll see you at dinner," he said as he bowed and tipped his hat before hurriedly retreating down the walk.

When he returned for the noon meal a few minutes before twelve o'clock, he found several men dressed in rough clothing sitting about on the porch waiting the call to eat. They nodded in a courteous manner to Mal and one of them moved forward and extended his hand.

"How do you do," he said, speaking in a deep resonant tone. Mal thought it was the most

pleasant male voice he had ever heard. "I'm Grady
Rogers."

"And I am Mal Smith," Mal informed him.
"I came in last night and am staying with John
Gurney."

"Yes, Mrs. Morgan told me," Grady replied.
Then he introduced Mal to each of the other men.
When the ringing of a small bell from inside announced the meal was ready the men filed through
the side door into a large room. A long table and
chairs nearly filled the room. The table was covered
with a blue and white checker cloth and laden with
bowls and platters of food. When each man had
occupied his usual place there seemed to be no
space left for the stranger. Evidently the person who
set the table had made a miscount and Mrs.
Morgan was greatly flustered.

"I don't know how that happened," she
muttered more to herself than to the man who stood
without a place. "I told Elly to set ten places."
She stopped and quickly counted the plates around
the table.

"Ten," she summed aloud. "Then there
must be eleven men. I do declare! I don't know
how I made such a mistake."

It began to look to Mal as though the situation was going to prove too much for Mrs. Morgan,
who apparently was so embarrassed over the slight
incident that she was unable to make ready another
plate. By this time, however, Grady Rogers had

picked up his plate and silver and stepped over to a small table at the side of the room.

"The big table will be a little crowded with another guest, Mrs. Morgan," he said quietly. "Mr. Smith and I will sit here. Now, will you bring another plate and silver, please?"

While she went to the cupboard to secure the service, Grady placed a chair for Mal opposite his own at the little table.

"Here you are, Brother Rogers," Mrs. Morgan sang out brightly as she handed him plate, knife, fork and spoon. "Now you can return thanks and everybody can eat." She was again in command of her household and no one could have felt more secure.

The men dropped their heads and Mal again took notice of the fine deep voice of this man who prayed with such simplicity and sincerity. They were served by Mrs. Morgan and the young girl who answered the door when Mal knocked earlier in the day. Great platters of fried chicken, mashed potatoes, cream gravy, lettuce, green onions, wild greens, hot cornbread and butter were placed before Mal and before he knew it he was eating heartily.

"So you are a minister?" he observed to Grady pleasantly.

"Yes," Grady replied simply.

"Here to fish?" Mal inquired.

"No, I live here."

"Oh!" Mal said in the way people have of using that interjection which might mean anything or nothing. As a matter of fact, Mal didn't know what else to say. His interest was genuinely aroused in the man sitting opposite him. Rogers seemed so much at home here and yet he had an unmistakably metropolitan air.

"Mrs. Morgan told me that you had come here to do some fishing. Is this your first trip to the Ozarks?" Grady inquired.

"Yes, I plan to do some fishing and this is my first visit here. It's really beautiful country."

"I am glad you like it. But then, how could you help it? We've got everything here — beautiful scenery, splendid fishing, wonderful climate and simple living among the finest people on earth!" Grady responded enthusiastically.

"Tell me, does every native Ozarker take a salesman's oath to sell this country to every stranger he encounters?" Mal laughingly replied.

Grady smiled his appreciation. "No," he said, "we don't take an oath. But we are all so happy here that we are anxious to share our blessing with others. However, I'm not a native Ozarker."

"No, I thought not," Mal said simply.

"And why did you think not?" Mal's companion asked.

"Oh, I've seen a few of the natives. John and Dave Gurney and the driver of the mail car. Also several customers at the post office yesterday. You're different."

"Yes, I suppose I am different, but it certainly doesn't mean I'm any better," Grady Rogers replied. "In fact, I can think of no greater fortune than to look and act and think exactly like one of these native Ozarkers."

"That so?" Mal seemed surprised. "Why? I've always sort of understood that they were more or less ignorant and lazy."

"Your education has been wrong," Grady replied seriously. "The Ozark people have been grossly misrepresented by the movies, cartoonists, postal cards and even books, but they really are the finest of the world's people. I like their basic philosophy of life, their practical faith in God and His goodness, their indelible belief in the democratic principles of social justice and the fairness and the contentment they find in the simple way of life."

Mal nodded meditatively. "You make it sound like something that the American people have lost in the past few generations. Something that was possessed by our pioneer ancestors that is not inherent in this age of knowledge and sophistication."

"Exactly," Grady responded. "These are people of pure Anglo-Saxon heritage and are the last seed bed of that great pure strain. The isolation imposed upon them by the ruggedness of these mountains has kept them unchanged all these years."

"But has the war not brought changes?" Mal inquired.

"Oh, yes, indeed," Grady hastened to explain. "I was referring to a period before the war. And even prior to pre-war days. The popularity of the automobile and the coming of good roads has greatly modernized life here."

"And the telephone, radio and newspapers too, I suppose," Mal suggested.

"The telephone has made little difference. The topography here is not conducive to building telephone lines. In fact, many communities such as this are as much as thirty-five miles removed from the nearest phone. But nearly every home has a radio and that, of course, has brought the outside world much nearer, especially since the war began and news of the fighting is so important. Still, almost no daily newspapers are distributed to these isolated sections."

Grady's companion gave interested attention as the preacher continued. "The war, naturally, has been a great force in creating a new life here in the Ozarks. Changes are being made that I hate to see. Our young people have gone to the far corners of the earth to fight in a battle that they had no part in creating. Others have gone to our largest metropolitan areas to work in building implements of defense. Too many of them will return saturated with a desire for the pleasures of a complex civilization. We'll see it reflected in the new life in the community, I'm afraid."

"On the other hand, there surely will be some good that will come from their association with new ideas," Mal said.

"Certainly," Grady readily agreed. "Much good. Many of the people who have gone away will return with money they have saved and will build good homes and improve their farms. The standard of living in general will be higher. That, of course, is fine."

Both men had finished their meal. Now they sat talking over cups of coffee after the others had finished and left the house. Mrs. Morgan and the girl called Elly began clearing the large table.

"Don't you all mind us, Brother Rogers," Mrs. Morgan said. "Just go ahead and visit as long as you want and don't pay us no mind."

"That was a very nice meal, Mrs. Morgan," Mal said politely, "I enjoyed it very much."

"Her meals are always good," Grady praised. "That's a point in favor of the Ozarks I forgot to mention. Goodbye, Mrs Morgan and Elly. We'll see you for supper."

The two men walked outside. Mal Smith turned to Grady and said, "I've enjoyed talking to you, Mr. Rogers. If you eat here regularly I suppose I'll be seeing you again."

"Certainly," Grady asserted, "and I hope your stay here in the community is a pleasant one and you'll find the fishing good. Tell John 'howdy.'"

The two men had reached the front gate and since each had plans in opposite directions they parted with a brief "goodbye."

chapter 7

MAL SMITH spent many hours of the next few days of his life fishing in the cold and sparkling waters of Spring River. When he was not fishing, he employed the time with long hours of tramping over the wooded hills. At bedtime his body was so weary from the exercise and his mind so filled with the wonder of this glorious country that he fell to sleep readily and awakened fresh and relaxed.

Mal and Grady Rogers had many pleasant visits as they met from day to day at Mrs. Morgan's boarding house. One morning as they ate breakfast Grady said he planned to fish that day. He invited Mal to go along with him. The invitation was eagerly accepted.

"Good," Rogers responded, "we'll start at ten-thirty. I have a little hike to take over the mountains. Have to see a man who is sick. However, it is only four miles and won't take long."

"A four mile hike to see a sick man!" Mal exclaimed. "You need a car."

"I'm afraid a car wouldn't be of much use in this case," Grady laughed. "The place is almost inaccessible. The road is rocky and rough all the way and the last half mile is only a foot path down across a hollow and up a steep bank."

"Does he live alone there?"

"No, his wife lives with him. As near as they can tell they are each eighty-six years of age. Neither can read nor write and the old man is almost blind. Their son was at church Sunday and said he was sick. I promised I would go to see him this morning and he will be expecting me."

"Do you mind if I go along?"

"Not at all," Grady answered. "I shall be very glad to have you. Then you can see for yourself why the use of a car would not be practical."

The two men set out at once and Mal soon found that he was going to have difficulty keeping up with this fast-paced preacher. Neither man talked much as each one seemed busy with his own thoughts. Grady paused several times to point out beautiful scenes from especially good vantage points.

The two men came into a clearing. In the center stood an old, two-room cabin. There was only one outside door and both rooms had small windows on each side. The door was flung wide open and there was no screen door to barricade the flies, pigs or chickens. Each of these annoyances made entrance into the house at will, but only the flies were allowed to remain. The pigs and chickens were shooed out without apology.

A feeble, elderly man and his almost-as-feeble wife greeted Grady eagerly. They explained to him how much they regretted not being able to attend church services.

"Sure do miss your preachin'," the old gentleman said, "but me an' the old woman's not much count no more."

"Your boy, John, told me you were not feeling very well," Grady responded. "I told him I'd be over to see you today."

"Yes, he told us you were comin' and we was a lookin' for you. I sure have been ailin' lately. Can't figure out what's wrong with me."

Mal Smith was introduced to this Ozark couple by his companion. They acknowledged the introduction politely with a "pleased to meetcha" accompanied by the inevitable handshake. From then on, however, Mal was completely ignored by his host and hostess, though not deliberately. They were just so completely engrossed with the visit of their friend, the preacher. As for the stranger with him they accepted him because he undoubtedly was endorsed by Brother Rogers, else they would not be traveling in the same company.

While Mal did not enter into the conversation, he certainly did not miss any of it. When he heard the elderly gentleman remark about his condition Mal noticed the purplish flush of his face and mentally diagnosed the condition as hypertension. He wondered vaguely how he might call Grady's attention to this apparent apoplectic tendency, when he heard him inquire with a note of anxiety in his voice, "Just how do you feel, Uncle Jim?"

"Oh, I'm plumb give out all the time," was the complaint.

"Do you ever fall?" Grady now wanted to know, much to Mal's relief. The preacher evidently knew what was probably wrong.

"He certainly does," the little old wife answered before her spouse could speak. "He fell one day last week out in the yard and has been so stove up ever since that he can hardly get out of the bed."

"What caused you to fall?" Grady asked, looking directly into the face of the man he addressed as Uncle Jim.

"They wasn't no cause for it," was the answer, "I went out to split up some cookin' wood so the old woman could can up some apples that fell on the ground after that hard rain last week. When I leaned over to pick up the axe I just toppled plumb over on the ground and a big pole fell on top of me."

Grady Rogers rose from his chair and laid a hand on the old man's shoulder. "Uncle Jim," he said sternly, "there is nothing the matter with you that a doctor can't fix up in a hurry. I guess we'd better arrange to have one visit you."

"Oh, I ain't had a doc look at me for more'n twenty-five years," the hillman protested. "Hain't never believed in them much. But once way back yonder I had quite a spell of the fever and Old Doc Fletcher come and stayed with me five days. He saved me, too. He's dead now and I hain't had a doc since. Don't know that there are any docs in this here country no more."

"There are good doctors in Hartstown," Grady Rogers assured him, "and I'm going to get one over here to see you tomorrow."

"But that would take a pile of money," Uncle Jim objected. "Let's wait until I get a little steadier and I'll get up and go over to see the doc. Reckon I can go on the mail hack from Clear Springs."

"No," Grady said sternly, "That won't do because you are not going to get any better until you get the right kind of medicine to keep you from having those dizzy spells.

"Keep him in bed, Martha," he continued, addressing his hostess, "and I'll be back tomorrow with the doctor."

"I sure am grateful for you coming over," the old lady said. "I've been uneasy about him for quite a spell and I've been a tellin' him he needs a doc."

Good-byes were exchanged and the two men were again on the trail. Silence fell between them until they were on the main road where they could walk side by side. Then Mal waited for Grady to open the conversation, although he was anxious to seek the answer to several questions.

"I'm afraid Uncle Jim won't be with us much longer," Grady remarked, "unless something is done for him soon."

"I'm sure you must have suspected hypertension from the questions you asked," was Mal's response.

"There's scarcely a doubt of it, but I don't want to trust any of my guessing or theirs about it. He needs professional advice and treatment. But left to make his own decision in the matter, he'd never get it done. His wife and children are just as helpless in such things as he is, so there was no use in a discussion. I'll get a doctor over there tomorrow and he'll be glad I did."

"But who will pay the doctor?" Mal wanted to know. "It's so plain to see they have no means."

Grady smiled to himself and said, "Your evidence is not conclusive, Lawyer Smith. When the doctor visits Uncle Jim tomorrow he will have the cash to pay him in full and he will do so without grumbling."

"But how do they manage? He has no earning power and surely he couldn't have saved enough to provide for his needs now."

"It is more likely than not that Uncle Jim has not been completely broke in the last fifty years. One of us from the outside can scarcely understand it, but most of the people here except the few families who are strictly improvidential manage to stow away a little savings against the proverbial rainy day."

"But what does the couple we just visited live on?"

"They have a cow and a few chickens which

help some, but for the most part they depend upon old age assistance."

"Oh, to be sure," Mal replied. "I had forgotten that the long arm of our generous Uncle Sam reaches even to such remote areas. And a very good thing it is I should say."

By this time the two travelers had retraced their steps until they were within a few yards of the trail that led to Grady Roger's small cabin. Grady suggested that they stop at his place for a refreshing drink of spring water and to pick up his casting rod. Mal felt that a brief rest would be welcome. It had been many months since his last army training. Although he had lived ruggedly while being protected by the French underground his muscles were not nearly as well seasoned as those of this hardy missionary preacher.

From Grady's place they proceeded to John Gurney's where Mal picked up his fishing equipment.

"Now, let's go by the Post Office," Grady suggested, "I'd like to see if there is any mail and I also need a new supply of hooks, sinkers and flies."

"Sure thing. I have everything I'll need except a pocket knife. Maybe Mr. Gurney will have some."

"Knives are his speciality," Grady declared as they entered the store.

"Dave," he continued, "Mal's in the market

for a knife. While you wait on him I'm going to look over your supply of flies and things."

"Just help yourself, Brother Rogers," the large bodied storekeeper said. He spread a sample of several patterns of knives from his liberal collection on top of the glass counter. He stood tensely by as his customer examined several of the knives before finally selecting one of medium size with good quality and a bone handle.

"How much for this one?" he inquired.

"A dollar and six bits," Dave spoke intently.

"I'll take it," said Mal reaching for his billfold and handing the merchant two one dollar bills.

Big Dave lumbered to the cash register with Mal following on the opposite side of the counter. "Plumb pleased you chose that knife," said Dave. "Didn't think I could be wrong about you, but sometimes a feller makes a mistake."

"I don't know what you mean," Mal declared in a puzzled tone.

By that time Grady Rogers joined them, the band of his hat decorated with a gay assortment of colorful flies.

"Count them, Dave, and put it on my bill," he ordered. Then to Mal he said, "Dave means that he has a theory about selling knives. He thinks he can tell a lot about a fellow by the kind of knife he buys."

"I sure can, too," Dave boasted. "I learn a lot about a feller just watchin' when he buys a pocket knife. Now you take a honest, hard workin' feller buyin' a knife. He picks a good solid one that will last a long time. And he's careful not to pay too much. A lazy feller wants a showy knife, light and sharp because he spends a lot of time just a whittlin'. And a bad feller wants a big knife with only one long blade—he don't pay the other blades no mind."

"That's very good," Mal responded and Grady hastened to add, "Now see what Dave means? The knife you picked is not big and ugly nor light and showy, therefore you fall in the category of the honest, good for something sort."

"That's sure the way I had you figgered all the time," Dave complimented, "and this just goes to prove it."

"Thank you very much, Dave," Mal responded without being aware that he had called the merchant by his given name. "I certainly do appreciate your confidence."

Grady ordered bacon, eggs, crackers and four slices of thick cheese for a lunch for himself and Mal, who remonstrated, saying he felt he should buy the lunch.

"No, you are my guest today. Now do we have everything? How about your license? Dave can fix you up."

"I have one," Mal replied. "The hotel man in Hartstown reminded me I would need it."

"Okay then, we're off. Dave, see you later."

chapter 8

WHERE DO WE GO?" Mal asked as they stepped out into the road in front of the Clear Springs post office.

"We'll go up near the large spring where Spring River starts. The season is closed on bass now, but it's open for trout. They're plentiful in the river below the spring. The water there is much colder and that's what trout like," Grady said as the two men swung along through the wooded hills. They were following a well worn path. In less than an hour they were walking down a long slope to stop on a level plot of blue grass by the side of the rapid mountain stream.

The stream was wide and clear at this spot and the two of them began preparing their casting rods.

Grady waded out into the icy cold water, closely followed by Mal. "We need hip boots, Grady," he shouted. "I didn't dream this water was so cold."

"You'll get used to it. But boots do help a lot."

They each selected a choice place for casting and began fishing earnestly. Grady was a master hand at casting and although he had an old rod the flies he selected in turn from his hat band landed within inches of the target.

Mal stood on a flat-topped rock in the rushing cold water, and swung his live dragon-fly bait as far upstream as possible. The fly floated and bobbed up and down as it followed the current. He had the first strike on his fourth swing. It was a two pound trout, strong, fast and game. Grady Rogers stopped his own fishing to watch with admiration as his companion landed the catch in a capable, sportsmanlike manner.

When he had seven and Mal four, Grady suggested they stop and get dinner.

"Fine, I'm famished," agreed Mal, "and it's a joy to be really hungry again."

They waded out to a large flat rock that flanked the river and placed their fishing equipment in a safe place.

"I'll build the fire," Grady offered. He was thoughtfully silent as he built two small walls about eighteen inches high of flat stones. Mal's statement, "It's a joy to be really hungry again," had a meaning for this discerning preacher whose hobby it was to know and help people. *Here's a troubled soul,* he thought, *burdened and suffering in silence and whatever his problem is he is trying to run away from it.*

Grady had done a great deal of wondering about Mal Smith ever since the man had come to Clear Springs. In spite of many subtle attempts to get Mal to tell about himself, he had learned nothing, except the bare facts that he was an attorney, had been in the war and had a medical discharge. It had taken a great deal of devious questioning to gather even those simple facts. Not that Mal was evasive. He was simply terribly reticent. Though he asked few questions and volunteered little information about himself, he still could not be called a dull conversationalist.

There was something in the quiet reserve of the man that caused Grady to respect his reticence. In their chance conversation he asked for no more than Mal was willing to contribute about himself and his life. But Grady was aware from their first meeting that Mal was unhappy. It was in the tiredness of his voice, in the painful troubled concern of his countenance. More than this, it was in the pitiful, hurt look deep in his dark eyes.

Something has hurt and wounded this man badly. And it is not his experience in the war. This is some personal injury that has cut him to the quick, Grady would think while he and Mal sat talking, usually at Mrs. Morgan's boarding house. *I respect his apparent desire to keep his own counsel.*

Thus each was glad to be in the company of the other on this day of fishing. Mal stood near the fire to dry his clothes. His interest mounted as the preparations for the outdoor meal progressed.

"How will we cook bacon and eggs?" he asked. "You have no pan or skillet."

"Aha! I was hoping you would ask. Now if

you'll be so good as to bring me a large handful of that yellow clay beyond you, I'll show you how to fare sumptuously in the woods without benefit of frying pan."

Mal walked over to the spot where Grady had pointed to the clay and looked gingerly at his hands before plunging them into the gummy substance. *Oh well, they'll wash and there's no shortage of water,* he thought as he dipped up a double handful of the yellow mass. This he carried back to Grady who had gutted the two largest trout by now. Grady packed the trout with a complete covering of the cohesive clay and placed them beneath a bed of live coals in the small stone furnace.

"We put the fish in first because it takes them the longest time to cook," Grady explained. "Now for the eggs. I'll bury them here in this small sand bar about two inches deep." Then with a flat stone which he selected for a scoop he carried live coals from the fire which he dropped over the submerged eggs.

He then cut a dozen green sticks about three-fourths inch in diameter and set them obliquely in the ground so that they slanted over the fire and the top of each stick was directly over the glowing bed of coals. A slice of bacon was fastened to each stick and the hungry men had nothing more to do except watch the sizzling meat curl as rich drops of fat sputtered into the blaze. An appetizing aroma permeated the air, tantalizing them. Since bacon cooks rapidly they were soon rewarded.

"Here you are, Mal," his host exclaimed as he handed him a crisp strip of hot bacon. "And it's my guess you'll like it. There's no food so delicious as that cooked over an open fire in the woods. But first, a word of thanks, please."

Mal did not enter into the prayer but he respected Grady's devotion and bowed his head.

"Where did you learn this sort of thing?" Mal inquired as they ate heartily of sizzling bacon strips and crackers.

"Boy Scouts. I was master of a troop for a number of years during my teaching days. This kind of thing takes me back."

Mal remained silent. He was curious about Grady Rogers. *Where had he come from, why was he here? What was in his past that caused him to come to this isolated section as a missionary preacher and teacher?* Still he refrained from asking questions. He appreciated the fact that Grady was probably wondering some of the same things about him, but had the good grace not to inquire into his life. Surely he could respond with the same consideration and delicacy.

While the two men sat eating, Mal saw a tumblebug rolling an earthen marble larger than itself. "What is that bug wrestling?" he asked.

"That's a tumblebug. It's egg is in the center of that ball. It is rolling it to form an earthen shell to protect its future child."

"Looks like quite a burden for so small an insect."

"Yes, isn't it. Makes one think of humans and their burdens. Many a person is carrying a burden as large in proportion to his strength as the one that tumblebug carries. The chief difference is that God helps man to carry his cares while the bug must go along with his until nature releases him."

"What about the man who has no faith in God or has lost the little that he had?" Mal's voice held a trace of bitterness.

"Then he is 'of all men most miserable,'" Grady quoted. "Every man in this life has some burden or responsibility, some less, some greater, but the size of the cares is not so important as his faith. Without faith he has no hope and it is hope that springs eternal in man's heart that makes life's load lighter. Even the bug does not live in vain."

Grady prayed fervently that he was saying the right thing to help Mal Smith.

"What do you mean, it doesn't live in vain?"

"The larva in that ball is called 'Scarab' and was symbolic to the ancient Egyptians. The life in that earthen ball meant to them the immortality of the human soul. It was the symbol of resurrection. A sign of pregnancy, fertility, reproduction and of life to come. The dead body, though buried in the earth, was to become a living soul. To the

Christians, of course, that is the hope that makes life glorious and very much worthwhile."

Mal was meditative and made no answer. Grady went back to his cooking. He removed the clay rolls containing the trout from the fire by the aid of two sticks tied with bark to form tongs. The hot clay was now baked to a thick brown.

"Here, crack them open with a sharp rock," Grady ordered as he deposited them on top of a flat rock. While the perfectly browned fish were cooling, Grady produced salt and pepper and two forks from his jacket pocket.

"Ah, a bit of civilization," Mal teased. "I was wondering if you would turn out a perfectly baked fish in clay shells tastily seasoned with salt and pepper."

"Which only goes to prove that the civilized way is the best way," Grady rejoined. "Only we need to be on the lookout that it doesn't cheat us of some very important factors."

"Such as?"

"Such as independence, individualism, self-reliance and integrity," was Grady's studied reply. "How does the fish taste?"

"Delicious!" Mal declared and then added, "I haven't had the eggs yet. How about them?"

"Coming up," Grady informed triumphantly as he began to dig in the sand. "Crack them and eat them."

The meal finished Grady carried water from

the river in his felt hat to extinguish the fire and Mal joined the brigade.

"Forest fires are pretty bad when they get going," Grady said. "They burn for days and often cause a great deal of destruction."

"Does any of this timber belong to the government?" Mal inquired.

"No, this is all privately owned, but it's all the more reason why a fire shouldn't get started, because here we're not blessed with government patrol and fire fighters."

"Well, I guess you don't have much danger of fires getting started this time of the year when things are lush and green," Mal offered as they picked up their fishing equipment.

"No, not now. The fire season is over for a while, but early in the spring the farmers set fire to the leaves in the woodlands and then things can get out of control."

"But why do they purposely set fires?" Mal wanted to know.

"They believe it rids the woods of ticks and snakes."

"And in exterminating those pests they rid themselves at the same time of the best soil enrichment — rotted leaves, as well as their best prevention of soil erosion and disastrous floods."

"Aren't the pages of your history filled with the disasters that have befallen man when he has operated in opposition to the laws of God and nature?" Grady added, "Let's go upstream a little

ways. The fishing is no better but there is some
beautiful scenery."

They soon found a well defined path that
led through the woods close to the stream. As they
walked silently along single file with Grady in the
lead, Mal began to hear a steady, dull roar. Finally
he called Grady's attention to the unusual sound
and asked what it was.

"That is the spring," Grady informed. "We'll
walk further up and you can see it."

When they reached the source of the roaring
noise, both men stood silent for several moments as
they gazed at the grandeur and perfection of God's
creation.

"I never saw such a spring," Mal exclaimed.
"It must flow millions of gallons of water in a year's
time."

"Yes," his companion agreed, "and a good
reminder to man of the omnipotent power and
mercy of God."

"Does the spring flow a steady stream the
year around or is it seasonal?"

"It is more or less constant," Grady explained. "That's one reason why the river has such
a consistent level. Another reason is the thing we
were talking about during lunch. That is the deep
bed of leaves in these woods act as a sponge to soak
up rainfall and keep the water from running off,
carrying a load of soil with it."

"What is that bright green vegetation growing in the water? I saw some in the water at the spring at John Gurney's."

"That's water cress. There's a lot of it here in the Ozarks. It's found in the cold, running water of the springs. It's good in salads."

The men left the spring and returned to their fishing. By midafternoon they had their limit.

"This has been a most enjoyable day for me," Mal declared as they walked back to Clear Springs. "What shall we do with these fish?"

"Why not take them down to Mrs. Morgan and ask her to serve them this evening for your supper there."

"That's a good idea," Mal said. "It's legal for a fellow to eat his own catch even if they have to be cooked at a boarding house."

"Right you are," Grady agreed. "Now, I must be going home to arrange to go to Hartstown tomorrow for the doctor. That means I'll not have Saturday to work on this week's sermon so I will have to do some studying tonight."

"By the way, we have Sunday school and an hour's worship at Stony Point each Lord's Day. We'd be happy to have you join us," Grady invited.

"Well, I'll think about it," was Mal's evasive reply. Grady knew he would not be there. He wondered why.

chapter 9

MAL WAS HARDLY ABLE to understand himself as he lay on his cot, after having eaten a
satisfying supper of fried fish and hot cornbread
at his boarding house. He had enjoyed the day
as much as it was possible for him to really enjoy
anything. He certainly felt grateful for the complete absorption of his attention so that he had no
time for his own unhappy remembering. But
at the same time he felt slightly irritated with
Grady Rogers. He couldn't exactly say why. In
fact he didn't analyze it as an irritation, but at
least something that was less then completely
satisfying.

He's such a religious fellow, Mal thought,
and yet he certainly hadn't been offensive. And he
hadn't given expression to anything either by word
or deed that merited fault-finding.

Mal had been in the Ozarks for two weeks
now and life was beginning to be a little easier for
him. Instead of eating, sleeping, walking or talking
automatically because it had to be done but with
no pleasure involved, he was now beginning to find
pleasure or displeasure even in the routine activities
of living.

From the beginning Mal had liked the
people of the valley. Slow and easy-going John

81

Gurney, whose nature was big and generous toward every one; his brother Dave, who was every bit as generous but more discerning of the faults of others; Grady Rogers, always kind and considerate, going miles out of his way to do some gracious act for his fellow being; and yes, fussy Mrs. Morgan, who cooked and served delicious meals even though her curiosity about the affairs of others sometimes got out of control.

These were about the only individuals who peopled the community that Mal had seen. He had, however, heard a great deal about Rosie and Hiram Jackson from John Gurney.

Usually when Mal returned evenings from Mrs. Morgan's boarding house he could find John sitting in front of his cabin listening to the quiet, subdued sounds of the night. He would invite Mal to sit with him and they would talk — or rather John talked and Mal listened. He was beginning to develop that habit with everyone. But to John it did not seem to make any difference, because he was not particularly interested in exchanging ideas with anyone. He did not seem to care a whit about what had happened to a person in the past — that is, he did not seem to worry about the things that a man was not ready to tell. All John wanted was someone to listen while he told tales of the past. Stories about his girl, Rosie, and her husband Hiram Jackson.

John's talk was too slow and tedious for attentive listening or repartee. But Mal only listened with half of his mind and the rest was reserved for his own brooding. He had little to say to anyone at any time so John's company proved to be quite satisfactory to him.

John, like nearly all Ozarkers, had long had the habit of retiring at an early hour. Mal had learned to recognize his none too subtle indications that bedtime was at hand. Whereupon he would say "good-night" and saunter off to his own cabin.

When Mal first came to the Ozarks, he usually threw himself fully clothed across the bed and lay there staring into the black darkness, his brain too benumbed with the shock of all he had lost to allow for thinking or reasoning. Gradually, however, the numbness began to wear off and reason returned.

Finally one night Mal reached a decision. He went back to life's beginning—his parents. He had had a good start there. Later had come his education, which though purchased through much sacrifice, had also been good. Then his marriage to Kathy. How wonderful it had been! He had loved her completely. Although she perhaps had not loved him so much, they were fairly well adjusted and for the most part happy. The building up of his career to a successful practice had been a part of their lives to which they both devoted themselves, although each with a different purpose and aim. He had prayed for success so that he could occupy a useful place in the community and so that his parents could feel that their efforts had been fruit-

ful. He wanted to be successful to make life secure
for himself and Kathy and their children. And more
than all else he desired success for the good feeling it gave him in regard to himself — self-esteem,
self-respect — call it what you like — Mal wanted
to be able to say that he had undertaken a task and
had performed it well. Then came a war. A
blundering, bloodletting, heartbreaking, cruel war
that tore men from their homes and transferred
them into a strange land to fight there for something that was not even clearly defined. And in this
particular war Mal lost much — his faith in things
eternal, his passion for loyal service, his health, his
happiness and, more than all else, his home. What
else was there for a man to live for? Yet life
must go on.

He began to consider what new endeavor he
could take up. None of the professions appealed to
him and all for the same reason — he did not want
a life that thrust upon a man many social en-
gagements for which he, Mal Smith, had no liking.
That was the one thing in his life with Katherine
that caused him more discomfort than anything
else — the constant round of parties and dances.

"It's disgusting, Kathy, to pretend to enjoy
a behavior that is shocking when all of the time
you are either bored or ashamed or both. That's
scarcely being honest with one's self, is it?"

But Kathy would only laugh and say he was
shocking himself — shockingly stodgy or old-fashioned, but she loved him just the same.

So in choosing a new life Mal knew he was going to steer clear of any vocation that would whirl him into a social merry-go-round. Besides Mal knew that if he chose any of the professions he would have to obtain specialized training. He was too eager to plunge himself deep into hard work to wait for training.

The only thing Mal had ever seriously considered as his life's work other than law was farming. As a youngster he had spent many of his summers on the farm of his uncle in Kansas and it was there that he learned to love the soil and animals. He was especially attracted to the production of beef on the ranges.

He used to remark to his uncle, "There is sense to raising cattle. They pay back to the soil what is removed by crops, they contribute an essential part of man's food and at the same time are very profitable. I hope some day I can own a ranch and raise beef cattle."

He never lost the ambition entirely. It had been difficult for him to make a decision whether to be a cattle rancher or lawyer. Finally he chose the latter, believing that if he became a financial success, he could invest in cattle and besides being a lawyer he could also have a ranch. Although the day had not arrived when he could have both he had never ceased to dream about it.

He knew that it was out of the question to go into ranching business now, because if he sold everything he possessed and used all of his savings he still would not have enough for even a small beginning in such an industry.

The next morning when Mal reached Mrs. Morgan's boarding house for breakfast, Grady Rogers, who usually ate only the evening meal with her, was sitting alone at the side table where he usually preferred to eat. Mal sat down opposite him and Grady explained he had come for an early breakfast so that he could catch the mail car into Hartstown to get the doctor for Uncle Jim Leatherman. But before they had finished eating, one of the old man's grandsons came looking excitedly for Grady to tell him that there was no need to go for the doctor as "grandpop" had had quite a spell during the night and died just at the break of day. The boy was riding horseback and stayed only long enough to give Grady the message. The minister promised he would hurry to the home as soon as he had finished his breakfast.

When the two men were again alone, Mal inquired, "What now? It is impossible to get an ambulance in there. How will they manage?"

"Why don't you come along and see?" Grady suggested, not so much because he wanted this stranger's curiosity satisfied but because he knew Mal needed the satisfaction of giving himself in service to others. He needed to see and feel the great need in this humble, saddened home and to lend a part in easing the burden there.

"But it hardly seems right," Mal objected. "Won't they resent an observer?"

"I don't want you for an observer, necessarily. There is much to be done and you can help."

"Oh! In that case I shall gladly go along." Mal could not help being attracted to this man of God in spite of the fact he felt slightly uneasy in his presence.

"Good," said Grady downing his coffee. "We'll start at once."

As the two foot travelers walked along again over the same trail they had traversed only the day before, the lawyer found it much more difficult to keep pace with the preacher who now was concerned with the urgency of the situation.

Mal was curious to know just what the procedure would be in this case of death in a home. Grady never seemed to be talkative while he walked and especially was he apparently pre-occupied this day. Mal decided to ask no questions.

They completed the four mile hike in less than an hour and when they reached the tiny log house several men and boys were standing about in the yard. Two of the men, sons of the deceased, and their wives were in the small house. Mal had never met Hiram Jackson, but when Grady introduced him to the neighbors and relatives gathered he noticed Hiram was one of them.

As soon as the greetings were completed Grady declared to one of the sons that he had come to help in any way he could. The man, who was past sixty years of age himself, said, "You'd better talk to Ma. She's in the house," and he led the minister toward the house.

Mal remained outside until his friend emerged again. "Aunt Martha wants the funeral day after tomorrow," he informed the persons waiting about. "You know, of course, it is impossible to get a vehicle of any kind to the house. So we'll make a litter and carry the body out to the road. Hiram, if you could drive your truck up to the place out there where the road forks we could have the ambulance from Hartstown meet you at the main road."

"All right, Brother Rogers," Hiram readily accepted the job assigned to him. "But does the undertaker at Hartstown know about all this?"

"Yes, they sent word over there as soon as Uncle Jim died. You know several members of the family live over that way. One daughter lives in Hartstown. Whoever comes for the body will inquire for instructions at Clear Springs. Someone will have to hurry right over there and direct him to the spot where we'll meet him."

"Danny can go," one of the Leatherman sons spoke up, referring to his fifteen-year-old son standing near by. "He has his horse here."

The boy had sprung into his saddle and whirled his horse into the trail before his father ceased speaking. Hiram Jackson was already walking rapidly away in the other direction.

"Now, men, we'll make a litter and get

started so we can be out to the trail when Hiram gets there. It's about five hundred yards."

Turning to one of the tall sons Grady said, "If you'll get us an axe, Jake, we'll cut down a couple of poles."

"Sure," responded the man named Jake. "I'll fetch it," and he strode off to a spot near an old shed where he found the axe right where his father had left it the last time he was able to use it. "Pa always kept a sharp axe," he praised as he returned to the group of men. "I've heered him say, 'many's the time that about all a feller really needed to make a good home was a good axe, a tea kettle and the Good Book to guide him.'"

"Maybe that was all it took when Pa was starting out, but it sure takes a powerful lot nowadays," a brother retorted. "My girl has been dingin' me about getting her hair curled up like some of the girls she seen at school. And yesterday I give in to her. Cost four bucks, but looked like she couldn't be happy without it."

The two brothers had insisted upon cutting the small poles needed to carry their father's body out to the road. Mal stood helplessly about feeling very much out of place until the poles were ready. Then Grady ordered him to help make the litter by spreading an old blanket upon the ground and placing one of the green poles at a point about one-third the distance across the width of it. This third of the blanket was folded over the pole and the second pole was placed lengthwise near the edge of the folded part of the blanket to hold it secure. The third of the blanket left over was now turned over the second pole and the litter was sturdy and safe with three thicknesses of the blanket.

Grady motioned for Mal to pick up one end of the poles while he took hold of the other end of the litter and they marched into the house. The neighbor men gathered in the yard trailed after them.

The body of Uncle Jim was gently moved to the litter and covered with a sheet. Members of the family stood about the room while neighbors performed the task. Then a neighbor took his place at each end of the litter. The poles extended three feet beyond the litter basket where the body rested. Using the extensions as handles the two men reverently bore the body down the steep slope to Hiram's truck.

Two days later the body was returned from the funeral home in Hartstown to the community church for the last rites.

chapter 10

A FEW DAYS LATER Big Dave sent Mal word that he wanted to see him. When Mal presented himself before the merchant Dave came directly to the point.

"I got a letter from a feller back East that has a place to sell. One hundred sixty acres of land. Part of it's broke out and they ain't no buildings on it except a two room cabin. It's made of hewed logs and it's real good. I jist 'lowed maybe you'd like to have it."

"How far is it from Clear Springs?" Mal inquired.

"Just short of three miles, an' he's only askin' a couple thousand dollars for it. That's dirt cheap the way things are a selling now."

"I don't know," Mal demurred. "By the time one paid for fencing it the cost would be a lot more."

"It's already fenced," Big Dave said.

"Oh, is that so? I thought most of the land around here was a part of the open range."

"Well, lots of it is," Dave explained, "but this fencin' was done by the fellers whose land joins it. Hiram Jackson, he's my brother John's son-in-law, joins it on the north and John Hillcroft has the land on the south and west. The east end fronts on a bluff above the lake and don't need no fencin'."

"Well, I've been toying with the idea of buying a piece of land here and this may be something I'd want, although it is not as much land as I had in mind. How much is timber?"

"Well, most of it is," Dave answered. "And some of the finest trees you ever saw, too. But they's about twenty acres a layin' next to the lake that has been cleared and broke out."

"That would take a lot of work," Mal interposed.

"It shore would. But you'd have two of the best neighbors a body could wish for. I reckon Hiram and Hillcroft would be as good help as you could get to clear your land."

"I'm going to take a look at it, Dave," Mal said, "and I'll need someone to direct me. Can you get away to go over the land with me?"

"John Hillcroft lives there hard by and he kinda keeps an eye on the place. He'll be glad to show you the boundary lines. He's mighty anxious to have a good neighbor get in there. Do you know where Hillcroft lives?"

"No, I don't believe I do," Mal answered.

"Well, you take the road right along the ridge goin' south. It's just beyond the ford, first house. You can't miss it. John's a fine feller and he'll show you all over the place. That would shure go fine with John's farm, but he told me he didn't want no more land with his boys gone to the war."

"I'll look the place over and let you know," Mal promised as he turned to leave the store. "If its convenient for Hillcroft I'll do it this afternoon. See you later."

It was not quite noon when he arrived at Mrs. Morgan's, but he asked that good lady if he could have an early lunch. He knew full well that she would cheerfully oblige, asking only that her curiosity be satisfied. She would want to know the nature of a mission that would cause him to ask for an off-hour meal. Mrs. Morgan was never disturbed if her guests ate early or late, but she was always anxious to know why.

"Elly fetch me that ham an' a couple of eggs from the refrigerator," she ordered in response to Mal's request and set upon her campaign to learn his reason. "I'm a fixin' Mal's dinner early."

Then to her guest she said, "You must be a goin' fishin' again."

"No, Mrs. Morgan, I'm not. I just decided to walk up the south ridge road and see the country," Mal returned.

"Hmph! Most folks don't get in such a worrisome hurry just to take a walk," Mrs. Morgan sniffed and Mal knew she was offended. Before he could think of a helpful explanation, his hostess continued, suggestively. "Them Goodman girls ain't at home. Or leastwise Ann ain't, cause

I seen her a goin' by here horseback wearin' britches just like a man. The hussy."

"I don't know the Goodman girls," Mal informed their assailant. "Do they live on this ridge, too?"

"About a mile the other side of Hillcrofts. But them girls ain't much good. Ann's bold as brass — and Mary! Well, I guess Mary's just as bad or worse, only she seems more decent like. Just slyer I reckon though! They are good ones to leave alone if you want my opinion."

Mal wasn't particularly convinced by Mrs. Morgan's opinion, but he refrained from saying so.

In an effort to appease Mrs. Morgan's ill temper, he told her that he was going up to see the Hillcrofts.

"Well, Grace Hillcroft might be at home," she said tartly. "School's out now. She teaches, you know."

"No, I didn't know," Mal said politely. "In fact, I didn't know there was a Grace Hillcroft. I'm going up there to see Mr. Hillcroft and it seems most likely that he will be at the house during the noon hour. That is the reason I asked for an early lunch."

Mal's inquisitor lapsed into an unexpected silence and he finished the lunch she had set before him during their chat.

"Thank you very much for serving my lunch early, Mrs. Morgan. It was very kind of you to go to the trouble," Mal said, rising from the table.

"No trouble at all, Mal. Elly can get this stuff all cleared away now before the rest come in for their dinner."

"Then I'll see you at supper time," Mal said, slipping a fifty cent piece under the edge of his plate. Then he turned and left the house.

The day was beautiful. Bright sunshine warmed Mal as he walked along. The call of birds filled the air with melody. Mal paused time and time again on the high points along the ridge road to gaze across the beautiful wooded hills and clear lake. A sense of peace filled his soul.

Just before coming to the Hillcroft cabin Mal found it necessary to ford a small stream that was a tributary to Spring River. Dubiously he removed his shoes and socks and rolled up his pants legs. Then he stepped gingerly into the clear water which was shockingly cold against his tender skin. Soon his body temperature became adjusted and Mal enjoyed a feeling of bold adventure as he stepped from one submerged stone to another.

When he had stepped from the last stone on to the shore, Mal sat upon a boulder and pulled his shoes and socks back on. Then he walked rapidly up the path to the Hillcroft cabin.

The oak door to the front room was opened to Mal's knock by a neatly dressed young woman whom Mal judged to be in her thirties. She was tall and angular, dressed in a severely conservative style. Her chestnut brown hair was fine and curly and no doubt would have been a glorious crown of beauty if it had been permitted to frame her not unpleasant face with its natural waves. Instead, the curly wisps were drawn straight back and held rigidly in place with an imprisoning net. The sallowness of the young woman's complexion was emphasized by this disciplined hairdress and her light colored, thick rimmed spectacles.

This must be the school teacher daughter, Mal thought as he introduced himself.

"My name is Mal Smith. I'm looking for John Hillcroft. Does he live here?"

"Yes, sir. He lives here. He's eating his dinner. Won't you come in?" she invited.

Mal entered the low-ceilinged, neatly kept room and followed his hostess into the kitchen were a man and woman sat eating their noon meal.

"Dad, this is Mr. Smith who wants to see you," the young woman explained.

John Hillcroft rose from his place at the table and stepping forward extended his hand.

"Right proud to meet you, Mr. Smith. I heard you been staying in Clear Springs this spring. You ain't had your dinner I reckon. Fix him a place and hotten up a cup of coffee," John ordered and returned to his place at the table.

Mal explained that he had eaten, but his gracious host insisted that he "set up to the table and drink coffee with them, nohow," indicating a chair. Mal reasoned he had to sit some place and since no other chairs were available he resisted no more and sat at the table. A huge wedge of pie was placed in front of him as well as a large white china cup of steaming black coffee.

Neither of the women was introduced to him and Mal was later to learn that it never seemed to occur to a man of the house to explain to a stranger who the women in the house might be. However, Mal recognized sad-faced Mandy Hillcroft as one he frequently saw lined up at mail time at the Clear Springs Post Office.

"I came to you, Mr. Hillcroft, to inquire if you could show me the piece of land that lies between you and Hiram Jackson's place."

"Well, now, I can't think of no reason why not," John Hillcroft replied, not without a trace of curiosity in his voice. "Hit belongs to a feller back east somewheres. Used to come here to fish. He made a deal with Dave Gurney several years ago to look after hit, but Dave's so busy in the store that he don't have time to get over here very much so he got me to mosey over there once in a while just to see that folks don't tear up the cabin or cut off any of the timber — lots of good timber on that place."

Mal nodded and opened his mouth to speak as his host crowded a huge bite of pie into his mouth. Before he could say a word, however, Mr. Hillcroft had raised his coffee cup to his mouth, had gulped down the pie, his mouth washed clean with the black liquid, and continued his praise of the farm.

"That there's a good piece of land. And the spring is the best one in the whole country. Nice snug cabin — two rooms and built good."

"How about the barn?" Mal managed to inquire.

"Oh, the barn is a big one. Just as big as the farm and roofed with the sky," the hillman boomed, a merry twinkle in his eye.

"John, you ought to be ashamed," his wife objected. "You know there ain't nary barn nor another building but the cabin on that farm."

"Daddy is always teasing, Mr. Smith," the girl referred to as Grace explained, smiling indulgently at her father. "You won't mind, though, when you get to know him. Are you planning to rent the cabin out?"

"No," Mal answered. "I understand the place is for sale and I might buy it if it suits me."

"Oh," Miss Hillcroft exclaimed, "how very nice. Then you will be our neighbor."

"I'll probably be a very poor neighbor," Mal remarked, "I'm not a very sociable person."

"Oh, he will be won't he, Father? You must come over often. Father likes company, don't you, Father?" said Miss Hillcroft.

"Are you a married man, Mr. Smith?" Mr. Hillcroft inquired.

Mal looked up and found all three persons about the table looking directly at him as though vitally interested in his answer. The attitude of tensity in the room was disconcerting. He answered the query with a simple, "No."

The host arose, "Was you aimin' to look that place over today?" he inquired. "If you are I can go over there now as good as any time. I ain't doin' nothin' much except clearing out some bottom land."

Mal rose from the table and followed his host out to the back porch where the man picked up his hat. Then they started down the path that led away from the Hillcroft cabin. Mal had not had an opportunity to answer the question asked of him, nor to express his gratitude to Mrs. Hillcroft and her daughter for their gracious hospitality. He was learning, though, that many such things were taken for granted in the Ozark country.

"What they askin' for that farm? Or did Dave tell you?" John Hillcroft asked as they walked along. "About two years ago the feller that owned it came here to fish and said he'd take fifteen hundred. I'd a bought it then, but it looked like all my boys was a goin' to have to go to war and sure enough they did too."

"How many boys have you?" Mal inquired.

"Three. All of them overseas now," John replied, his voice betraying no emotion to show what his feeling was in the matter. "What did you say they are asking for this land?"

"I didn't say," Mal replied, reflecting that he hadn't been given a chance, "but Dave told me the owner will take two thousand dollars for it. He seems anxious to sell it."

"That's probably on account of the war," John Hillcroft mused. "'Tain't so easy nowadays to travel. And folks ain't got much time for fishing vacations either."

"That's quite true," Mal agreed.

The two men had reached a wire fence along which they walked for a distance of a quarter of a mile. It was a good fence set with solid oak posts and three strands of tightly stretched barbed wire.

When they came to the end of the boundary line they crossed over the fence and spent most of the afternoon walking about the one hundred sixty acres lying there. John pointed out the saw timber, the spring, and the level bottom land bordering the wooded lake. As they were walking deep into the wooded section of the farm, John stopped beside a large white oak and examined a fresh axe mark upon the tree.

"What do you know?" he said. "Some polecat has marked a board tree. I wonder who done that."

"What do you mean by 'board tree'?" Mal asked.

"Why a tree they can use to split boards for a new roof," John explained. Then noticing Mal's lack of comprehension he explained further. "Er, that is roofing shingles. Some fellers split them by hand, you know, from white oak."

"But how do you know that is the reason this particular tree is marked?" Mal inquired.

"Because anybody that knows a board tree when he sees it, knows this is an extra good one. The thievin' cur that notched this one most likely wants to sell it. And they bring a right smart piece of money."

The cabin proved to be sixteen feet wide and thirty feet long when measured on the outside. It was well built of handhewed white oak. The builder had erected it on a stone foundation two feet above the ground. The floor of the garret rooms above formed a beam ceiling that lent a charm to the low-ceilinged living room. A substantial fireplace at one end added to the beauty and comfort of the room. It was of hand cut gray stone and had been erected by an expert stone mason.

"What a beautiful fireplace!" Mal exclaimed. He had visions of a cheery fire casting shadows on the plain knotty pine boards that finished the walls of the room. "The man that built this place knew something of comfort and coziness."

"Yes, I reckon he did," John agreed. "I recollect when he built this here cabin. I tried to talk him out of building that fireplace. A stove's a heap handier. We used to have a fireplace, but I closed it up and set up a heating stove. Takes less wood and holds fire longer."

Mal wondered vaguely why a man that lived where wood fuel abounded would be so economical with it, but he really was not listening attentively because his mind was busy calculating the furnishing of the cabin with the antique pieces that had been left to him by his parents.

"This here cabin's a good one," John Hillcroft opined. "Look at that floor. It's two inches white oak. They ain't no crack between them boards."

They went outside and John said, "That roof's getting pretty bad. Needs new shingles. A couple of fellers could cut and make enough boards for a new roof in three days. Then it would take two days to put them on, I reckon. Be a heap cheaper that way, but you'd probably rather buy roofing shingles in town."

"No, as a matter of fact, I don't think I should," Mal answered. "I'm as anxious to save a dollar as the next one and I believe I'd prefer a board roof."

"Well, I guess you have seen it all, Mr. Smith. I'm plumb sorry about that board tree," John lamented as though he was personally responsible to Mal for the happening. "I'd say this was a plumb good place for the money."

"I agree with you," Mal said, "and I'm going to tell Dave I'll take it. I thank you for showing me around. Since Mr. Gurney will receive a commission, no doubt, for executing the sale, I'm sure he will offer you a fair amount for the time you have taken to show me the place."

"Oh, sure Dave will take care of that. Only there won't be no pay because Dave has accommodated me many a time. Back a few years ago times was pretty hard and Dave just about kept everybody going in these parts, me included. I'd have to do a heap more than this before I can ever pay Dave back for all he's done for me."

"Well, I certainly do appreciate your help, Mr. Hillcroft. I'll go back as far as your place with you and then I'll go on to Clear Springs and arrange to buy the place."

Mr. Hillcroft talked loquaciously as they walked over the trail to his small cabin. Mal scarcely heard, so busy was he making plans to occupy his new home and engage in the business of earning his living from the soil.

When they reached John's cabin he pressed an invitation for Mal to come in for a more prolonged visit. Mal declined because he was anxious to get to the business he had on his mind.

They parted at the front gate but Mal had gone only a few paces when John called to him.

"Say, if I was you, I'd go over there and cut down that board tree before somebody else gets it. Its the best one on that farm, or in this whole country, for that matter."

"Thanks," Mal replied. "Thanks a lot, Mr. Hillcroft. I'll see about it right away."

chapter 11

As HE WALKED rapidly toward Dave Gurney's store, Mal decided that he would go back home and dispose of all his property and furniture, reserving the treasured pieces that had been in his mother's family for several generations and enough kitchen utensils to make his new home comfortable.

When he reached the store only the proprietor was there. He loked at Mal expectantly. "Well, did you'uns see the place?" he inquired.

"I sure did, Dave. And I'm going to buy it. There is not as much land as there should be for a good farm, but I like the location and the cabin. It's a honey."

Dave was encouraged with Mal's display of enthusiasm, something that no one had observed before in the stranger.

"Now ain't it, though," Dave responded. "A hundred sixty acres ain't much land but a feller can grub out a nice easy living from it, especially if he don't want too much. And that cabin was really built for good living. Especially for a man what ain't got a woman, 'cause it don't take no sight of housekeeping to make it clean. Say, I never thought to ask you before. Maybe you got a woman. Are you married?"

"No, I'm not," Mal answered flatly. "And I

don't expect to grub out a living on that farm, Dave. I expect to plan and work and make that place pay me good money for my labors. I've been doing a great deal of studying and thinking along this line since I've been here and it has been my observation that you people here don't use the right methods. You still think along with your grandfathers that the only way to get any returns from this soil is to plow it out. Well, that's all wrong. This ridge land is not conducive to row crops. There are several reasons for that — the contour of the land, the depth and quality of the soil, the size of the fields and inaccessibility to markets. That all makes row crops unprofitable."

Dave looked hurt and defeated. "Sure, I know," he said. "This part of the county can't brag much about its soil. It's pretty rocky and all, but it's a good place for living. A man don't need much — a good comfortable cabin, plenty of good food and enough clothes so he can keep clean and warm. I reckon most folks has about all they wants here in this country and they don't have to work too hard to get it neither."

"But a man should expect to work hard to get what he wants from life. Especially in this day when there is so much competition," Mal argued.

"Cain't see no need for a man to drive himself when he can get all he wants without it," Dave added irritably, "and they ain't no competition here. Every man sets his own groove and goes along in it without bothering about the other feller, except maybe to give him a helping hand once in a while when he needs it."

"But what about the comforts of life?" Mal inquired.

"We got comforts a plenty," Dave answered. "Fox hunts at night, fishin' for sunny days and the best of God's creation to look at with plenty of time just to set and think."

"I mean things to make life easier and more pleasant like radios and electric lights and washing machines and gas cooking stoves — things for your womenfolks."

"Well, I've always noticed," said Bachelor Dave, "that the more you give a woman, the more you can keep on giving her. They's been lots of girls gone away from here to get work and when they come back they are all painted up like silly dolls, got unnatural curls in their hair and wears britches just like a man, and some even smokes cigarettes. Now they are restless and don't want to take care of their children and keep pestering their husbands for more things — comforts, I reckon you'd call 'em."

"It's the modern way," Mal explained, "and it seems to me its about time the women of the Ozarks began to get a little pleasure out of life."

"Pleasure!" Dave exclaimed. "Hmph! Was a time when a woman found pleasure a plenty raising a fine family. So you think you want that farm, eh?"

"Yes, I'll give you a check on the Hartstown Bank for two hundred fifty dollars to seal the bargain," Mal said, drawing forth his check book. "I have enough money in the Hartstown Bank to pay for the place and if you wish you can go with me to the bank tomorrow and I'll put the rest in escrow to be paid to the owner when I receive a warranty deed and abstract of title that shows clear ownership."

"No, the two fifty will be enough," Dave replied. "I'll send it on to the feller that owns that place and he'll send back the deed. Your check will be your receipt."

"Thanks, Dave. I'll go home now and get ready to go to Hartstown tomorrow. I suspect I'll be gone several days."

Mal returned to his cabin and brought out the suit of clothes that had been hanging neglected all these months. He found it necessary to brush it vigorously. He laid out a fresh white shirt, tie, socks and shoes.

He would go early the next morning on the mail bus to Hartstown and from there return by bus to his home town to dispose of all his property and the belongings that he would never again need.

When his clothes were ready and his small bag was packed it was time for him to go to Mrs. Morgan's for his supper.

Grady Rogers and Mal customarily lingered at the table over extra cups of coffee after the other guests drifted from the dining room. But tonight the preacher was absent. Mal, knowing his habits, concluded he was probably busy holding a religious service in some nearby community or was away on one of his endless missions of mercy to his fellow man. Mal felt a twinge of disappointment, for he was anxious to report to Grady that he had purchased a farm and that he was going to take up residence in the Clear Springs community.

Since Grady was not present he debated whether or not to confide in Mrs. Morgan or just to announce to her as he left the house that he was going to be gone for a few days and let her inquiring mind find out the reason in the best way she could. Just then, that good lady came into the dining room and said, "Mr. Smith, I found this here half dollar on the table by your plate when you left today noon. I reckon you must a dropped it."

"Why no, Mrs. Morgan, I didn't drop it," Mal replied, making no move to take the coin as it was extended to him. "I left it for you as a tip."

"What do you mean, tip?" inquired Mrs. Morgan disapprovingly.

"Well, it is like this, Mrs. Morgan," Mal explained. "In the cities when a waitress brings a customer the food he orders in a cafe or restaurant she expects the customer to leave a bit of change on the table when he leaves to pay for her services. So today when I asked you to go to all of the extra trouble of preparing me an early meal, I left the the half dollar to sort of pay you for your trouble."

"But don't them girls get paid for waitin' on customers by the fellers that own those eatin' places?" Mrs. Morgan inquired.

"Certainly they do, but its an old custom in this country that the person who buys the food should also contribute a small amount for the service."

"Well," said Mrs. Morgan, tossing the half dollar on the table in front of Mal's plate, "I'd say it was a poor way to do. You come here and pay me what I ask for the stuff you eat. It shorely stands to reason I ought to be willin' to set it before you decent like so you can eat it."

"I'm sorry," Mal began picking up the coin, "I didn't mean to offend you. I only thought to pay you for the accommodations I asked of you."

"'Tain't no offense, Mr. Smith, but now that you have bought yourself a farm and are goin' to live here, you ought to learn that folks hereabouts don't want no pay for the little things they can do for each other."

"Oh, so you know I have bought a farm?" Mal said, ever puzzled and amazed at the speed with which news traveled in this isolated spot.

"Sure," Mrs. Morgan answered naively, "I've been aimin' to go see Mandy Hillcroft for nigh onto a week so I just moseyed down this afternoon and they told me."

And I don't suppose you were prompted one bit by your curiosity about my visit there this afternoon, Mal thought ruefully. But to Mrs.

Morgan he only said, "I believe I have a very nice place there."

"You sure have," she agreed, "and you got it cheap too. It's the best built house in the country. When will you be a movin' in?"

"I am going to have to be gone for a few days before I can get settled," Mal replied. "I'll not be here for meals for a week or maybe longer.

"And then," he continued, "when I get into a home of my own, I suppose I'll be preparing my own meals."

"Breakfast and dinner maybe," Mrs. Morgan predicted, "but you'll soon be eating your supper here with me regular, just like Brother Rogers."

"Probably so," Mal laughed as he rose from the table. "Goodbye now, Mrs. Morgan, I'll be seeing you when I return."

The next morning Mal met the mail bus at the Clear Springs Post Office and rode to Hartstown. If he had not been so absorbed with his own problems and plans, he probably would have noticed that Dave did not greet him as effusively as he customarily did. But Mal was so preoccupied with his immediate problems that he failed to notice that Big Dave was more or less reserved.

In Hartstown after he had finished his business with the bank, Mal boarded a bus and traveled until he reached his home town the next day.

He went at once to the home of his father-in-law from whom he learned that Katherine was making a tour of the western states. Mal was grateful for that. He felt that the ordeal of separating himself forever from his former life would be easier if he did not have to face Katherine or her husband.

Judge Dalton told him that Katherine's baby, a girl, was three months old and was being cared for during the absence of its parents by the housekeeper in his own home. He asked Mal if he would like to visit the baby to which he replied, "Of course not. I'm here to get rid of my possessions I'll never again need and to get out of town as fast as I can."

"You apparently have some plans," Judge Dalton stated inquiringly, and waited for Mal's answer.

"Yes, sir, I have," Mal answered politely. "I realize there are legal procedures necessary to straighten out this unholy tangle. I shall put my part of the affair into the hands of my former associate, Attorney Bruce Blair. Kathy's lawyer can get in touch with him. Blair will know where to reach me, when the decisions have been made. It will not be necessary for me to appear in court."

"We have not known where you could be located," Judge Dalton said. "How could you have dropped out of existence so completely?"

"You can scarcely blame me for going away," Mal broke in bitterly.

"I know, I know," Judge Dalton hastened to explain and added. "As soon as Kathy and Neil recovered from the shock of your unexpected return, they went into court and declared themselves innocent parties. Since you were her legal husband, Kathy refused to live with Hamilton until some disposition was made of your marriage. I was anxious to make an attempt to find you so we could clear up the whole matter, but Kathy wouldn't agree to it. She said you would return some day and do the right thing."

"I see," Mal said inadequately.

"Kathy came home to live until her baby was born. When she regained her strength she became restless and two months ago went to California."

"And Hamilton?" Mal inquired hating himself for the asking.

"Well, he's behaving just like you would expect a man like him to react. At first he was so bewildered you couldn't help feeling sorry for him. Then he went away and was gone at the time Kathy's baby was born, when she needed him most. Later he returned, but when he is sober he is intermittently morose, sullen or abusive. Most of the time, however, he is intoxicated and more often than not dead drunk."

"I see," Mal again said as he stared abstractedly out of the window. Then he rose suddenly to his feet and said he must be about his affairs.

For the next two days Mal worked feverishly to dispose of all essential details that required his personal attention. He decided that since he would need some mode of transportation on his farm he might as well buy a good used ton and a half truck. He could pack and move all the furniture he wanted except such large pieces as two walnut bureaus, a cherry cupboard and small grand piano. These things he would have crated and shipped by truck to Springfield. Other smaller things which he wanted to pack himself he loaded in his truck. He instructed his lawyer that he wished Kathy to have any personal things that she desired and for all other property and possessions to be sold. The proceeds were to be divided equitably with Kathy.

Finally when the last bit of packing and planning was finished, he looked at his watch and noted the time was 5:30 P.M. There was still time for two hours of driving before nightfall, so he jumped into his truck and drove away without telling anyone goodbye or where he was going, with the exception of his lawyer and friend, Bruce Blair.

Mal drove about two hundred miles that evening before deciding to stop for the night. There was something good in speeding down the lonely road. It helped him to feel that eventually he could get so far away from memories and dreams of the past that he would forget all about any other life than the one that stood just off in the immediate future.

The experience of the past two days had revived emotions and memories in him that he had hoped were buried. After all, it had been four years since he had lived with Kathy. To be sure the one thought that had kept him going during the horror-filled days of the war was the hope of returning to Kathy to take up their life where it had left off. But he had learned to believe in the past few months of his isolation and solitude in the Ozark Mountains that the shock of finding Kathy lost to him forever had been a means of killing his hopes and dreams and burying his memories.

Now his return to his old home served to open the old wound and expose the hurt and injury, still raw and bleeding.

Only time and long days of hard driving work will effect the actual healing, Mal reasoned. When a healthy strong man works until he is physically exhausted he can go to bed and to sleep. When he awakes rested he can get up and start the hard work again. That is why I want this hill farm. It will take long arduous hours of labor to make the farm pay off. And I intend to make it pay. I never did have any use for half-hearted efforts. I want this farm to pay off in money and I want it to pay me in health and if not in happiness, at least in the satisfaction of having made a success of this new life I have chosen for myself.

chapter 12

THE DAY THAT MAL left Clear Springs, Grady Rogers came into Big Dave Gurney's store inquiring for him. "I heard that Mal has bought the old Sims place next to Hiram Jackson," he said. "Do you know anything about it, Dave?"

"I reckon I do," Dave retorted, "bein' as I'm the one that sold it to him."

"Oh, it is true then, Dave. I was afraid it was only hearsay. That is just the right place for Mal. He'll do all right there."

"Well, now, I ain't so sure he's gonna do all right any place," Dave said, "He's got a lot of fancy notions. And I ain't so sure I done right to sell it to him nohow. After all we don't know nuthin' about him. Why, do you all know, Brother Rogers, he ain't had a single, solitary letter since he come here. And he ain't mailed none either. Seems mighty queer to me."

"Well, you can hardly condemn a man just because he carries on no correspondence," Grady replied. "He has been through the war you know and it seems he just wants to live quietly and sort of think things out by himself."

"That's just it," Dave interrupted. "What things is he thinkin' about? As far as you and me are concerned we don't know what he's thinkin'."

"It's a free country, Dave. Mal fought to keep it that way, you must remember. A man has a right to think as he pleases," Grady said.

"I ain't forgettin'," Dave replied soberly. "But it just seems kinda funny him a comin' here like this. We don't know if he's got a family or how he makes his livin' or nothin'."

"I suspect the reason we don't know is because it's none of our business. We do know that Mal Smith seems to be a decent and honest fellow, who no doubt has his own reasons for keeping his affairs to himself," Grady lectured.

"I guess you're right like you usually are, Brother Rogers. Anyway, you cain't hang a man because he don't tell you all about hisself," Dave was in a more amiable mood now.

"And you know, Brother Rogers, I just cain't help noticin' how much better Mal is a lookin' nowadays. I felt plumb sorry for him when he first came here a lookin' so beat out."

"You're right, Dave. Mal is looking much better. That's why I am so glad he has bought a farm here because this kind of life will help him overcome the trouble in his soul," Grady contributed.

"You think he is troubled in his soul?" Dave inquired.

"Sure he is. I don't know what has happened to him and haven't tried yet to find out, but you just can't talk to a man as much as I have talked with Mal and not learn something of what goes on inside of him. And that is the biggest battle Mal Smith has to fight. He is not at peace with himself and God."

"Well, that ain't the way I got it figured," Dave persisted. "He acts to me like a body that has been plumb licked by something that has happened to him."

"We don't disagree there, Dave. I'm sure something has happened to him. Maybe it was his experience in the war."

Just then Hiram and Rosie Jackson came into the store where Dave and Grady were talking.

"Howdy," Hiram said, his nod including both of them.

Rosie, however, walked across the room and said, "Good morning, Uncle Dave," and extending her hand to Grady, said, "Glad to see you, Brother Rogers."

"We're all excited," she continued, "because we have just heard that Mr. Smith bought the old Sims place next to us. Is it true, Uncle Dave?"

"It sure is, Rosie," her uncle responded, "An' Mal has gone away for a few days. He gave me a check for a down payment on the Hartstown Bank and said he had enough money there to pay it all at one time if I wanted it that way."

"What did he go away for?" Hiram inquired.

"Well, now, he didn't say," Dave said, scratching his head thoughtfully. "We got to talking about other things and I didn't ask him why he was goin' away nor where.

"Come to think of it, Mal just ain't the kind of a feller that you go a askin' them kind of questions nohow," he continued.

"That's probably the reason we don't know much about him," Rosie said. "Maybe he's got a wife and family and has gone to them."

"No, he told me he wasn't married," Dave said, "but he didn't say nothin' more."

"He does aim to live here, doesn't he?" Rosie asked quickly.

"Oh, sure. He said he was goin' to be away just a few days. But he's comin' back and is goin' to live in that there house."

"Then," Rosie said, turning to Grady, "we'd better get it cleaned and ready for him, don't you think, Brother Rogers? There's been grain stored in that house off and on for several years now an' it's covered with dust and cobwebs and dirt."

"I'm sure Mal would appreciate having his new home nice and clean when he returns," Grady agreed, remembering how he felt when the same gesture of friendliness had been extended to him years before when he was a newcomer to the community.

"Tomorrow is Sunday, Rosie, so you can make the announcement in church."

"Yes, Brother Rogers," Rosie agreed, "and we'd better do the work Monday so it will be all ready when Mr. Smith gets back. All of us women will go and wash the windows and clean up the house and some of the men can rake away the weeds and grass and clear out some of the sprouts close to the cabin."

"That's a fine plan, Rosie," said Grady, "and how about lunch? Will we eat together?"

"Oh, sure, Brother Grady. Everyone will fix a dish of something and some sandwiches and we'll all eat together at noon out under the trees." Rosie was always enthusiastic about plans for such affairs. Then at once she subsided and added reflectively, "Only I wish Mr. Smith could be there with us. I've never seen him but once or twice and it seems to me, Brother Rogers, that he looks like a very sad man. Sorta like he had been bad hurt."

"Me and Brother Rogers was just a speakin' about that," Dave said. "But Mal is a lookin' better than he did."

"Maybe now that he's comin' here to live, he'll start comin' to church," Hiram said. "There's nuthin' that will do for a feller what a goin' to church will do. I've found that out."

"Yes," Rosie agreed, "if he'd only come to church and listen to some of your good sermons, Brother Rogers, he'd surely feel easier in his mind."

"If he'd only go to church, Rosie," Grady Rogers commented, "and worship God—he and all men on earth—he'd find not only peace in his soul, but he'd find strength and wisdom and faith to help him solve his problems or bear his burdens. If my sermons or discourses are helpful to the hearers, I rejoice in that for I strongly feel that a sermon should be helpful in causing people to live closer to God. However, the sermon is not the important part of the church service."

"It ain't!" Dave expostulated. "I always thought good preaching was pretty important."

"Me too," Hiram chimed in, "and Brother Rogers really preaches good."

"Brother Rogers says good preachin' helps," Rosie broke in, "but he was gettin' ready to tell us about something more important. Weren't you, Brother Rogers?"

"Yes. I believe the most important reason for going to church is to worship. This is done with singing, praying, meditating and listening together. But the greatest factor of worship is the attitude of the worshipers. When you deposit money in the bank at Hartstown you can take out only the amount you deposited plus the accrued interest; so it is with worshiping God. You can take away from church only what you put into the service, plus the blessing that God has put upon it."

"Then you don't really have to have a preacher at all for people to worship together, do you?" Hiram asked.

"Hiram, we knew that long years ago before Brother Rogers came here," Dave said. "We used to meet together and sing and pray and different people would take turns making a little talk about every Lord's Day when we didn't even have a preacher, except one that would drift in once in a while."

"I can remember those days," Rosie added. "But since Brother Rogers has been here, we don't know how we'd ever get along without him."

"The day is coming and not too far away when someone will have to take my place, Rosie," Grady said, "I'm not getting any younger, you know. I had hopes that your boy, Frank, would be recruited for the Army of the Lord before he was drafted."

"Rosie and me had the same hopes," said Hiram. "He's just nineteen years old now, you know. We sent him to high school and he was talking something of going off to school some place to learn to preach when he was drafted."

"I still believe he will be a preacher," his mother responded. "I pray for it all the time and I know God answers prayers according to His purpose. And I sure don't see no reason why He wouldn't want Frankie to be a preacher. Do you, Uncle Dave?"

"No, I sure don't, Rosie," Big Dave answered. "He surely must know that this here old world needs a powerful lot of preachin'. I've a notion if Frank wants to preach, the Lord will do His part in helpin' out."

Others came into the store and Dave was busy filling their orders for groceries and feed. Grady Rogers, who in all the years he had lived in this Ozark community had never been able to purchase an automobile, picked up his bag of supplies and started off down the trail to his cabin, walking briskly and with a characteristic buoyancy in his step.

His pattern of life, though varied with many tasks and performances of duties peculiar to his ministry to the people in this isolated mountain section, almost invariably included a trip to the store on Saturday morning from which he returned at nearly noon. Then after a light lunch, he would sit down to an afternoon and evening of reading and deep study and prayer to prepare the message for Sunday morning.

Rosie and Hiram followed the same pattern in their preparation for the Sunday morning worship. Rosie cleaned her house thoroughly on Friday. She had taught her three young daughters, who were now nine, thirteen and fourteen years of age, to perform all the duties of keeping the house clean, comfortable and healthful. While she and Hiram went to the store on Saturday morning the girls did enough baking and preparing of food to last over Sunday.

During the afternoon hours each of the women folk took a bath, shampooed her hair and set her clothing for the next day in readiness.

After the evening meal, instead of taking their family to Hartstown for a movie and an evening of social festivities as many of their neighbors did, Rosie and Hiram spent an hour or two studying the week's Sunday school lesson together.

As they explained to their children, if it was a good thing for children to prepare their week day school lessons it was even more essential to be prepared for a good Sunday school discussion period. Rosie also maintained that a person was much more refreshed and composed for helpful worship on the Lord's Day if the previous evening had been given to rest and quiet study.

At the beginning of their married life, Rosie and Hiram had established the habit of reading aloud from the Bible each evening after supper dishes had been cleared away. When their oldest child Frankie came along and began growing up, he was often delighted and showed an early interest in the stories and great truths he had learned from the Bible from the reading of his mother and the stories she told him daily. Later, as the three daughters were added to their family, the mother continued teaching quotations and stories from the Bible to them.

Rosie had been teaching a class of teen-age girls and boys in the local Sunday school for many years and now her oldest daughter under her mother's able guidance and encouragement, was teaching a class of primary children.

chapter 13

Mal Smith slept soundly the night he returned to Clear Springs and did not awaken the next morning until he heard a rap on his cabin door.

"Coming," he shouted in response to the knock.

"No need to open the door," was the answer and Mal recognized the voice of John Gurney. "I just come down to tell you to come over and have bacon and eggs with me. I heard you come in last night and I knowed you must be pretty tired."

"All right, John," Mal answered back, "I'll be over as soon as I get dressed."

By this time he was sitting on the edge of the bed reviewing in his mind the events of the past few days. His brain slowly went into action, putting each happening in the proper place, then raced on into the future. Mal was presented with many problems, immediate and future. Coming to this realization, he was galvanized into activity, although he felt tired enough to return to a state of collapse. In fact, upon awakening almost any morning, Mal usually felt that life would be so much easier if he could only go back to sleep instead of facing another day of loneliness and longing and hopelessness. A few times in the past few weeks he had tried that very method of escape only to find himself so wrought by the act of trying to sleep that such repose was impossible.

Now he bestirred himself and rapidly drew on his clothes. He found John Gurney sitting on his porch waiting quietly for his guest.

"Come in," he invited as Mal stepped up to the porch. "I'll fix a bite of breakfast."

With movements slow and deliberate, John provided Mal with a hearty breakfast of bacon, eggs and steaming hot coffee which Mal drank without benefit of sugar or cream.

In the meantime John rambled on, "I reckon you'll be movin' out of the cabin right quick now. I'm goin' to miss you a powerful lot. But I'm glad for you that you've bought that farm. Nuthin' like workin' in the open all day to make a man forget the things he wants to. Have some more coffee."

"Thanks," Mal seized the opportunity to speak while his host was preoccupied with the business of filling his nearly empty cup. "I had some furniture I wanted to move here so I decided the best thing for me to do was to buy a truck. I'll need it anyway."

"You shore will," John chimed in. "That's a lonesome place you bought, but not too hard to get to. I guess the road has kinda growed up though, 'cause it ain't been used for such a long time. When you aimin' to move?"

"Today," Mal answered draining his cup and rising from the table as though being reminded of the many tasks at hand. "I'll take the things that I have in the truck to the cabin and unload them. Then I'll have to clean out the dust and dirt. Perhaps I'll have time too, to run over to Hartstown for a mattress and stove and other things I'll need."

John was tempted to tell Mal that he need not worry about having to clean his newly acquired home, but he felt it would be much better for Mal to discover it for himself. Instead he inquired, "Will you be needing a hand? I ain't much account no more but maybe I could help you get some of that stuff unloaded."

"Thanks a lot, John," Mal replied to the elderly man whom he had grown to appreciate. "That furniture is heavy and I'll need a strong young fellow to help me. Do you know someone I might hire for a while?"

"Well, Hiram Jackson lives right there by you. Do you know him?" John suggested.

"Yes, I've met him. Do you suppose he could help me today?"

"Don't rightly know," John said slowly, "but he's likely at home this morning. You might stop when you go by his house and ask him."

"But I thought I'd take the road past John Hillcroft's place," Mal said. "It's shorter, isn't it?"

"It would be shorter if you could use the road that runs back of his place, but you'll find

you can go through a gate about a hundred yards
below Hiram's house that will land right up to
your cabin. It's a whole lot better road."

"Will Jackson object to me driving through
his place?"

"Course not," John replied. "And if he's
home he'll be glad to help you unload."

Mal thanked John and hurried across the
way to jump into his truck and drive toward his
home. As he passed Dave Gurney's store, he
stopped. He entered the building where he was
greeted cordially by the proprietor.

"Glad to see you're back," Dave boomed.
"See you've got yourself a truck. You'll be needin'
it. You musta come in sometime in the night."

"Yes, it was nearly midnight when I got to
bed. John gave me my breakfast this morning.
I'm going now to clean up my cabin and unload
the things I brought back with me. Guess I'll need
a new broom and cleaning powder."

Dave brought forth the requested articles,
although, like his brother, he would have enjoyed
telling Mal that his house had already been
cleaned.

"I wrote that feller you had bought his
place and he sent the deed and abstract for it,"
Dave said, drawing the document from a pigeonhole
in his battered roll top desk.

Mal received the papers and began to study
their contents. "It all looks okay," he said when he
had finished, "except I'll want to check the legal

description against a survey before the deal is completed. There is a public surveyor, I presume."

"Yes, he's over at Hartstown," Dave informed. "A plumb good feller too."

"Good," Mal replied. "I'll go to Hartstown tomorrow and arrange for him to make the survey at once."

"You'll find that description is exactly right," Dave said, "but I don't blame you for making sure."

"If I didn't feel very sure it was accurate I wouldn't even move into the house," Mal stated. "However, I do want to know for sure before the deal is closed."

Mal picked up his broom and made his way to the truck. When he reached Hiram Jackson's cabin he discovered the farmer turning his milk cows into the pasture. Hiram readily agreed to help Mal move into his cabin.

"Sure, I can help you," he said. "I ain't a doin' much today. I'll go down and open the gate and it'll be a pleasure to help you move in."

Once through the gate, Hiram took his place beside Mal in the truck and directed him in following the infrequently used trail to Mal's cabin.

As they came into the sight of the house, Mal thought he detected a different appearance about the surroundings, but he couldn't at once determine what it was.

"Well, here we are," Hiram stated genially when the truck was brought to a final stop.

"Yes," Mal answered, a puzzled look on his countenance, "But it somehow looks different — bigger and better." He looked quizzically at Hiram who was grinning broadly. "Let's go inside," he said, eager to see Mal's reaction to the transformation that had been wrought there.

Mal quickly alighted from the truck and Hiram followed him through the door into the empty cabin. A look of astonishment came over Mal's face with his first observation of the room. That look was quickly replaced with a heavy unpleasant scowl.

"I wonder what's happened here," he said. "This place was more like a barn than a house when I left."

"Rosie and some of the other women thought it needed a little soap and water," Hiram volunteered, "so they cleaned it up for you. They'd feel right bad if they knew you wasn't goin' to like it," he added.

"Oh, of course I like it," Mal brightened. He crossed the room and fingered the freshly starched curtains at the window. "It looks splendid and I did dread the bother of cleaning the mess out of this place. But your wife and the others — why should they go to so much trouble for the comfort of a stranger?"

"I reckon that's the reason they done it," Hiram replied ungrammatically, "because you're a stranger. They want you to know we're glad to have you move here an' we hope you won't be a stranger 'mongst us for long."

"Thank you, Hiram," Mal's feelings were mixed about this evident gesture of good will and neighborliness. He felt grateful to be relieved of the tedious and unpleasant job of cleaning his home, but at the same time he resented the invasion of his privacy. He was quite convinced that the whole affair presented a problem to be solved. He had always been a reserved person and his greatest pleasure had always come from delving into the contents of books or listening to good music. When neither of these diversions dispelled a siege of gloomy despair, the act could usually be accomplished with an hour or so at the piano.

For several weeks before purchasing the farm, Mal had begun to miss his books and piano. That was one reason he was so quickly persuaded to make the purchase once he had seen the house. Sitting high on a bluff above the beautiful lake that was so clearly visible from the spacious window across one side of the living room, the cabin commanded a mile and a half view of the placid blue green water, bordered on one side with the woods of native trees and shrubs.

The picture of ever-changing, ever the same, natural beauty of lake and countryside appealed to Mal. He felt he could more nearly find peace and contentment here with his books and music than in any place he had ever seen.

"Well, since the cleaning is already done,"

he remarked to Hiram, "we'd just as well get the things moved in. It won't take long and I'll have time to make a trip to Hartstown today to buy a stove and other things I'll need."

The two men worked fast and almost entirely without conversation. Hiram noticed that the few pieces of furniture were of fine quality and felt a little awkward and out of place in its presence. The bedstead especially caused him to stare. It was a huge old-fashioned thing of solid walnut. When they had it set up in the bedroom and the springs were in place, Hiram inquired skeptically.

"Did you say you were going to buy a new mattress in Hartstown?"

"Yes," Mal answered. "Why?"

"Well," Hiram drawled, "that looks like a powerful big bed to me."

Mal looked at Hiram and then at the bed, "I think you're right, Hiram," he admitted. "I sold the original mattress to this bed. The bed has been in my family for generations. Now I'll have to have a mattress made to order which will take some time."

He seemed perplexed at the problem and Hiram offered to lend him a bed until he could purchase a mattress.

"That's kind of you, Hiram, but I'll buy a studio couch for the living room and sleep on it until I can get this bed completed."

The last of the load was four large boxes of books which were so heavy as to cause Hiram to groan under their weight. "What's in them boxes?" he exclaimed as he tried to lift his end of them.

"Books," Mal said. "I'm sorry they are so heavy. Maybe I'd better unpack them first."

"Oh, no, I can carry my end if you can handle yours," Hiram was quick to say, feeling a trifle ruffled that his ability to perform with physical strength had been challenged. When the last box of books had been brought into the house, Hiram straightened up and wouldn't even allow himself the luxury of a deep breath to relieve the hard knot that had tightened within him due to the heavy exertion.

Mal stood several seconds fanning his brow with his hat and breathing heavily.

Hiram laughed indulgently, "Get your wind?" he inquired indifferently.

"Yeh," Mal replied, "I'm kinda soft I guess."

"That's an awful lot of books," Hiram remarked. "Do you read all of them?"

"I have read them," Mal replied. "And I hope to again and again from time to time. There should be plenty of opportunity for me to read here."

"Where you goin' to put all those books?" Hiram inquired, looking around the room. "I don't see no shelves."

"I thought I'd build shelves all along the walls on each side of the fireplace."

"Sure. That will be fine," Hiram responded

and then added wistfully, "It must be great to know all the things that's in them books. Sometimes a feller misses out a lot when he's not got a education."

Mal felt strangely drawn to this hillman, but was at a loss to know how to reply to this observation. To relieve the embarrassment he jammed his hat on his head and said, "I guess that's all we can do here now, Hiram. It's not quite time for lunch. I'll have time to drive to Hartstown and eat there. I'll drop you off at your house."

When he reached the county seat, Mal went at once to see the surveyor and made arrangements to have his boundary lines surveyed. He visited several furniture stores in an effort to buy a gas range. None was available. Each merchant simply asked him to place his name on a list and promised to let him know when a stove came in.

I might have known, Mal thought, but this was his first encounter with wartime shortages. Finally he purchased a small four-hole cook stove in the basement of a hardware store for twenty dollars.

"I'm not even sure though that there is a flue in my house," he explained to the merchant. "I've just bought the place and hadn't noticed if there was a place for a wood burning stove."

"If there is no flue, you can run the pipe out of a window or up through the roof," said the hardware man. "Lot's of folks do that and never bother to build a chimney."

"It doesn't sound very practical to me or

very safe," Mal observed as he paid for the stove.

He also bought a studio couch, platform rocker and small dinette set.

He now felt that he had enough equipment to start housekeeping and returned to his cabin.

When he reached the gate at Jackson's, Hiram was there to open it for him, "I'll go along with you to help unload the stove and things," he offered.

On the short drive through the timbered trail Mal narrated his experience in trying to secure the stove.

"I had a good gas range that I could have brought down here, but it seemed a better plan to sell it there and buy a new one to save transportation."

"Looks like somebody would have told you about things bein' hard to get," Hiram remarked. Mal reflected that he really hadn't asked anyone's advice about disposing of his things so great was his desire to get rid of his belongings so he could return to the Ozarks.

"Anyway, you can put yourself at ease about the chimney," Hiram continued, "'cause I know there's one there. I helped build it."

"Good," Mal returned, bringing the truck to a stop once more in front of his home. Quickly the two men put the load of furniture in the positions Mal selected.

Then he turned to Hiram and asked, "How much do I owe you? I don't know how I'd have managed without you."

"You don't owe me nothin', Mal. I've been proud to help you out."

"But I want to pay you. I insist on paying you. I can't allow you to work four or five hours a day for me for nothin'."

"Mr. Smith, folks hereabouts don't take no pay for bein' neighborly," Hiram said firmly. Mal returned his wallet to his pocket, but he was not pleased.

"Guess I'd better be goin' along. Soon be milkin' time," Hiram said, moving slowly toward the door. Before leaving the room he turned and said, "You've sure got a homely place here. All them books and nice things. I'd sure be proud to help put those books on the shelves when you are ready."

Mal paused a moment before replying. His neighbor's evident yearning for book learning was touching. But he didn't want help from anyone unless he could pay for it. However, he finally said slowly, "All right, Hiram, when I get the shelves ready I'll let you know."

chapter 14

MAL FOUND LITTLE TIME for loneliness in his new home after the first evening. The second day was like the first, filled with many tasks that needed to be done at once. So were all the succeeding days.

The first morning after he arose, made up his bed and ate his breakfast, he unpacked dishes, cooking utensils and the other small objects necessary for keeping house. These he put in their proper places and then methodically went about making a complete list of all the things he felt he would need, including the axe he couldn't do without as well as some kerosene lamps (he had found his way to bed the night before by the aid of a flashlight because he had forgotten to purchase a lamp).

The surveyor arrived at nine o'clock and they were busy until noon running the boundary lines. Mal was not surprised to discover they checked correctly with the legal description in the deed, but he felt it was worth the time and money to be certain.

After lunch he and Big Dave went to Hartstown to finish all of the details of the purchase and to record the deed. Mal made a long list of items to purchase in Hartstown, things which were not available at Dave Gurney's store. When they returned to Clear Springs, he hurried away to his cabin.

I'll do all I can to put things to rights here in the house, he thought, *then I'll check the fences to have everything in readiness for that truck load of heifers coming in day after tomorrow.*

By the end of the day, his housekeeping routine was efficiently established and all furnishings were in place except the books. That would have to wait until there was time to build the shelves.

From the second day onward Mal spent the hours from early morning until late in the day working on his farm, repairing fences, building a barn and chicken house. He had decided against raising hogs but made plans to accommodate sheep at some future date. All of this activity kept Mal so well occupied and physically tired that he had no time to be lonely. And the folk in the valley were saying he had no time to be "neighborly" either.

After getting his house arranged for comfortable living, Mal was first concerned with getting the fences in readiness for his cattle. He had purchased fifteen head of yearling Guernsey heifers and a registered bull to be delivered on the following Saturday morning. On the morning he started out to inspect the fences for necessary repairs, he met John Hillcroft coming to pay him a visit.

"Heard you had moved in," John said.

"Thought I'd mosey over to see how you're doin'. Maybe you are needin' some help."

"I've been moved in two days," Mal replied. "Hiram Jackson helped me unload. I brought some things back in my truck. Now I'm going to check the fences — I've got some cattle coming in Saturday morning."

"Well, I just came over to visit," John said, "so I can go along the fence with you. You might need some help. But you ain't got nuthin' with you to fix fences with. If I'd a known I could have brought along some —"

"I have tools with which to make repairs," Mal cut in, "but I'm just going to take inventory today and mark the spots that are bad. I'll come back later to repair the places."

"I never did see it done that way," John responded slowly. "We allus just take maul and axe and steeples along and fix up the hole where we find it."

"I believe I can make a better fence and save time this way," Mal said. "See, we'll begin in this corner. I have a notebook here and I'll jot down the location and a description of each repair needed. Then tomorrow I'll try to get two men to help me and we'll start making repairs."

"Well, now I'm not doing anything tomorrow. I could help as well as not," said John.

"Good. But first let us agree on the matter of wages."

"Oh, I won't charge you much. I don't work

out much. Just a little to help out a neighbor once in a while. I could help you with the fence and you could come over and help me get in my crop when it's ready."

"I shan't have time to help anyone else," Mal stated. "I'm going to be very busy here all of the time. So if you work for me, we'll have to agree first on a wage. What do they pay by the day here?"

"Oh, for fixin' fences — I'd say about three dollars," John Hillcroft said.

"Three dollars?" Mal exclaimed. "A man can't afford to work for three dollars a day. I'll pay you seventy-five cents an hour for eight hours work. What do you say?"

"Sure, that suits me," his neighbor replied jovially. "I done told you I'd help. But you're goin' to get in trouble paying that kind of wages. There's some fellow what owns ranches around here that ain't goin' to like it."

"I guess a man has a right to spend his own hard earned money anyway he likes," Mal said stubbornly. "I happen to believe in giving every man a living wage."

"'Course, I don't make my livin' at wages," John spoke ponderingly.

"But your time is valuable whether you are working for wages or working on your own farm — and you should be paid for it."

"Well, yes, if you look at it that away," his

neighbor agreed. "Anyways, I'll be glad to work for you at that price."

"Okay. We'll start at eight o'clock in the morning. I'll try to get Hiram Jackson to help also."

All in all, Mal found not less than a dozen bad places in the fence which he recorded in his notebook. As soon as the survey was completed he went to see Hiram Jackson who agreed to come the next day and help repair the fence.

"That's a mighty good wage," Hiram complimented when Mal explained the terms upon which he wished to hire help. "I'm plumb proud to get it, 'cause I always aim to hire out a few days every month to get some cash money."

"Then perhaps you can work from time to time for me. I plan to build a barn and chicken house soon and I'll be needing assistance. Do you do any building?"

"I sure do. I built my own house and barn. I like that kind of work."

"By the way, Hiram," Mal said, "I'll be needing to buy eggs, milk and butter for a while. Does your wife have a surplus that she could sell to me?"

"No, I'm afraid not, Mr. Smith. I milk the ten cows and sell all of the milk, except what we use for the table and cooking, to the cheese factory at Hartstown. We've only got about fifteen hens so I don't have spare eggs. But you can get them things over at Mrs. Goodman's."

"Oh, yes, and the Goodman's live about one-half mile further down the road than John Hillcroft, don't they?"

"They sure do. Mrs. Goodman and her two girls, Ann and Mary."

"And there's no Mr. Goodman?" Mal inquired.

"No. The family moved here to help build the dam before we had Wooded Lake. Mr. Goodman was killed on the job. The girls were little then. Mrs. Goodman liked to live here and the government gave her enough money to buy the place where they live besides a pension every month. She's run fattening cattle on the place and has done right good."

"And you think she could supply me with eggs and dairy products?" Mal repeated.

"Yes. She has a big flock of hens. Makes butter and cheese for folks that want it."

Mal called at the Goodman's cottage that afternoon. He was greeted by a young woman obviously quite different from most of the girls he had encountered in the valley. She stood tall and slender and relaxed. Her copper red hair hung loose and wavy about her oval face. Mal thought he had never seen more expressive eyes. Upon first glance they were blue and seemed to change upon close scrutiny to an indescribable green. Her white skin flushed with the healthy color of youth was perfect in combination with her hair and eyes.

The girl was neatly dressed in a white silk

blouse, green gabardine skirt with a green scarf tied in a bow at her slender white throat.

"I am Malcom Smith," the stranger introduced himself when his rap at the door was acknowledged. "I have recently bought a neighboring farm — the old Sims place — and am now living there. Neighbors told me that possibly I could buy supplies of eggs and dairy products here."

"Come in," the young woman invited. She lead him into a bright room filled with furnishings that had once been good but had now grown shabby.

A faded rug covered the floor. Crisply starched curtains and drapes at the windows with cretonne covered easy chairs and divan arranged about the room made it look cheery and comfortable. A small radio sending forth strains of popular music was resting on a little table beside a huge overstuffed chair and the divin was flanked at each end with tables upon which sat matching lamps. A tall reading lamp with a bright colored shade stood at the left side of another chair. (Mr. Goodman had wired this house for electricity, preparatory to the day when the dam would make electricity available). Along the wall opposite the divan stood an upright piano.

A young woman with a little boy three or four years old beside her sat on one foot upon the divan. She held in her hands a large picture book from which she apparently was entertaining the child with stories read aloud from its pages.

A middle-aged woman with iron gray hair sat in a comfortable rocker by the window. Her lap was filled with sewing.

The young woman who answered the door crossed the room and turned off the radio. Then turning toward the older woman, she made the introductions.

"This is my mother, Mrs. Goodman. I am Ann Goodman and this (turning toward the divan) is my sister Mary. This is Jody," she finished, smiling at the little boy.

How do you do's were repeated all the way around the room and Mal was assigned to the chair beside the radio.

He liked the homey atmosphere of this room and wondered vaguely about these women who made the home. Who played the piano? Where was the father of Mary's child? Away at war, perhaps? But Hiram Jackson had intimated that only the women constituted the family.

Mal repeated his request to Mrs. Goodman who answered affirmatively that she had eggs, butter, cheese and milk to sell. How much would he want?

"I'd like a dozen eggs today and a pound of butter. And I'd like to get a quart of milk each day," Mal replied. Mrs. Goodman commissioned Mary to prepare the order for him. Mary was not as tall as her sister nor was she as pretty and slender. But she moved with an easy grace that suggested cultured poise. She was dressed in a plain print dress the skirt of which was longer than her sister's. Her chestnut brown hair was simply arranged. Stray curls fell rebelliously about her full heart shaped face. The sisters resembled each other only in the smooth white fineness of their skin. Mary's eyes were brown and sad. The little boy had a head of curly red hair, with eyes of deep blue. Mal reflected that he resembled his aunt more than his mother.

He and Mrs. Goodman exchanged pleasantries while he waited. Ann had seated herself on the divan but did not enter into the conversation. Mal felt slightly ill at ease as she sat there. When he turned to ask her a question he found her gaze full upon him. Their eyes met and he thought he detected a bit of a challenge there. There was an inviting gleam of approval for her new neighbor. Or a bit of mockery. Perhaps it was only a slight show of curiosity. Whatever it was it lasted only a fleeting moment and she dropped her gaze.

"Do you play the piano?" Mal inquired.

"At times," she replied meeting Mal's gaze directly. And then added, "Why?"

"Oh," Mal was a little baffled and slightly irritated with her bold manner, "no reason. Usually," he added, "when there is a piano someone plays it. I just wondered which of you play this one."

"Do you like music, Mr. Smith?" Mrs. Goodman asked.

"Very much," Mal answered. "I play the piano. It is my favorite instrument."

"I taught both of my girls to play. Ann started when she was five years old. She learned quickly and we thought she'd go far in music but after a few years she lost interest."

"And Mary? Does she play?"

"We were so discouraged with Ann that it never seemed worthwhile to try with Mary," Mrs. Goodman said wearily.

By this time Ann had risen and walked arrogantly to the piano. She played a popular tune entertainingly, though with much improvisation. Finishing she scooted to one end of the piano bench and said to Mal, "Now it's your turn."

Mal laughed lightly and replied, "No thanks, I'm out of practice. Perhaps some other time."

Mary returned to the room with the eggs, milk and butter packed neatly in a small box which she quietly placed on the table. She didn't look directly at the stranger and spoke not a word, but her errand completed she retired quietly.

Mal paid Mrs. Goodman and said a polite "goodbye" to Ann, thinking he again detected a trace of mockery when he looked into her face.

What a world of difference in those two sisters, he thought as he walked along the trail home. One quiet, poised and plain looking, the other pretty, graceful and interesting — very, very interesting.

chapter 15

ANN GOODMAN was excited and pleased that
Mal Smith had come to Clear Springs to live now
that she had met him. She had heard of him ever
since he had arrived a few months before but their
paths had never crossed and she had not had so
much as a glimpse of him. This fact had not caused
her any disturbance because from all of the ac-
counts she had had of him she had concluded
he must be quite dull.

Ann herself had only returned to the valley
to live a few weeks before Mal put in his appearance. She had been brought up there as Hiram
Jackson had explained to Mal. Her parents had
come there when she was only four years old and
her sister Mary was a baby. When she was nine her
father was killed on the job while building the dam.
They had quarreled with relatives before coming to
the Ozarks to live, so instead of taking her husband
back to his home for the last rites Mrs. Goodman
had buried him nearby.

With the indemnity from the government
she was later able to purchase the farm where they
now lived and had managed to provide well for
herself and two girls with the monthly pension
awarded her.

Both girls had completed high school and

Ann had gone to college for two years. She had a teacher's certificate and a contract to teach in an elementary school. Then the war came along and defense work had offered much more money and excitement than a teaching career so she resigned her position and went to Kansas City to work in an aircraft assembly plant.

When Mary was graduated from high school, her mother persuaded her to wait until Ann was out of college and earning her own way, explaining that she was scarcely able to finance both of them in school at the same time.

Mary was disappointed for she was quite eager to continue studying, but she felt her mother deserved consideration in the matter. She quietly acquiesced to the plan, deeply hurt by her mother's apparent partiality.

In her heart, Mrs. Goodman felt that sending Mary to school would be a waste of money and effort because she had learned so slowly. Her report cards showed as good grades as Ann's but her teachers said she learned with a great deal more effort. Ann was the type of individual who seemed always to know the right answers with almost no effort. She earned a reputation as being an unusually bright pupil. That her fund of knowledge was oft times quite superficial never seemed to occur either to her mother or her teachers. Mary knew deep inside her that Ann was not a brilliant student, but she never at any time gave voice to her opinion.

When she found it necessary to postpone her college education Mary borrowed money from her mother and went into the chicken business. There was a large poultry house on the place that they had never used. It was there when Mrs. Goodman bought the farm. Mary had it repaired and installed electric brooders. Then she bought baby chicks, raised them to broiler size, dressed them herself and sold them to a large tourist hotel located in nearby Lake City. The work was hard but the profits were more than gratifying.

After about six months in the chicken business, however, Mary's mother became ill with an ailment that required surgery. She was in the hospital for six weeks and after returning home four months elapsed before she was able to leave her bed. Since it was necessary for Mary to give her mother constant nursing care the girl was compelled to sell her chickens. She also had to use the money to pay for her mother's expensive surgery and hospitalization. Only by the closest economy and privation were they able to keep Ann in school.

Whatever might have been Mary's feeling in the matter, she did not suggest that Ann come home to help with the care of their mother, for she knew Mrs. Goodman had her heart set on Ann's becoming a teacher. The family was having its first experience with financial difficulties and Mary was sure they would either have to sell some of their stock cattle at a sacrificial price or go into debt. Her mother, however, seemed not to be worried.

"Ann will be earning a good salary next year," she would say. "And then with her help things will be easier."

Mary was less hopeful, however, as she continued to care for her mother through the long weary months. It was more than a year before Mrs. Goodman regained her health sufficiently to care for herself and Mary could be freed from her responsibilities.

In the meantime Ann had given up her school. Characteristically she had gone to the city, secured a position and resigned her school before bothering to write anyone of her plans. This left Mary to break the news to their mother and to bear the brunt of her disappointment and depressed spirit.

At one time Mrs. Goodman had been a cheerful, gentle-natured individual. But through the lonely weeks of illness and pain, she had become quite petulant and cross. Where once she looked on the bright side of things she now complained at length about everything that happened to her. Where once she was gentle and kind she was now cross and demanding. Her optimistic disposition had grown neurotic and despairing. All of her faith in things better to come had become centered in Ann. Now that she was disappointed in that respect she grew quite morose.

Then came the war and the call for women

volunteers. Ann wrote she planned to enlist. Mrs. Goodman and Mary had a long talk about Ann. It was decided it would be best for Mary to go to the city and enlist with Ann.

Mary knew her mother would be better off if she had to depend more upon herself. The girl also knew that Ann would need her. Mary was inwardly happy for she realized she had been mistaken in thinking her mother considered Ann the more brilliant of the two. Her mother sensed that Mary's presence in the service with Ann would be a steadying influence. It never occured to her that the chances of them being assigned to the same division were decidedly remote.

Three years in the service went by and the two girls came home. Mary had married in the service. Her husband, a lieutenant in the Marines, was the son of a wealthy banker, the political boss of the state. They had a two-week honeymoon before he was shipped to the European theatre where he was killed at Normandy. Mary had been discharged when she married, but had taken a job in an airplane factory. She had contributed a substantial portion of her pay check toward paying the mortgage on the farm. She continued until Ann was discharged. They returned to Clear Springs when Jody was five months old. Mary's government insurance had taken care of the mortgage and had left a sizeable nest egg for Jody's education.

chapter 16

MAL SAW MARY AND ANN quite often after
that when he went for his daily quart of milk. The
marked difference in the dispositions of the two
sisters became more apparent as he came to know
them better.

He noticed that Mary was the more serious
and industrious of the two. During the early twi-
light after the supper hour was his usual time
for making the journey to the Goodman's. But
no matter when he reached the Goodman home
Mary was busy at the household chores, while
Ann never appeared to be definitely busy at any
task.

Not that it mattered in the least to Mal. He
was much too occupied with his own activities and
troubled thoughts to take any interest in the
affairs of others.

Still, Mary and Ann, each in her own way,
were keenly curious about Mal and what had
brought him to Clear Springs.

Mal was to learn much of the lives of the
two girls later, but for the present he was convinced that the best way to forget the hurt caused
by one woman was to stay away from all women.
Still, his attitude was not so much a willful re-

jection of the attentions of women as a complete unawareness of their presence.

Mary was not at all disturbed by Mal's reticence. She thought him a nice person and was especially attracted by his polite manners. A delicate sense of propriety kept her from being so bold as to show any undue interest in a total stranger — especially one who evidently had no inclination to share confidences with anyone.

Mal's seeming bewilderment at times and the hurt look deep in his fine gray eyes did not escape Mary, however. She often wished she knew what had happened to put that hurt look there, or what she could do to help if she did know.

Rosie Jackson was Mary's best friend and confidante and they frequently discussed Mal's coming to the valley. Both would have liked to help if they had only known what to do.

"The men don't take to him very much," Rosie remarked. "Hiram says he's not very neighborly and Uncle Dave called him a 'stubborn fool.' But I expect folks just don't understand him."

"Could be that he doesn't understand our ways very well either," Mary observed. "He seems like such a nice man it is hard to believe he really wants to be unfriendly."

"Well, Hiram and I have decided that we will be neighborly with him," Rosie said. "Can't see how it can do any harm and maybe some way we'll be able to help him."

Mal was not purposely being unfriendly.

He just was not giving any thought to his behavior toward his neighbors and fellow citizens in the community. His great reason for coming there was to find a way to forget Kathy and all she meant to him, including every phase of his former life. It was proving to be a much harder task than he had thought possible. He found balm for his tortured soul only in hard physical labor. So he was in the field with his tractor from the time of the first light of day until the evening shadows drove him homeward where he gladly laid his weary body upon a bed to rest for another hard day on the morrow.

Mal early discovered that Sunday, although it was the Lord's Day, offered no surcease for his tortured mind that became unbearably active with the long hours of relaxation. So he fell into the habit of creating jobs to help him through the day. Gradually he began making plans for a seven day week instead of six. Finally the time came when he scarcely knew the Lord's Day from any other.

Not knowing the facts concerning Mal's seeming disregard for the Lord's Day, his neighbors took it for granted he was an irreligious man and censured him for it. True, many families were careless in their adherence to all of the Christian teachings, but scarcely a native was so callous that he failed at least to rest "the brutes" on Sunday.

The regular church goer was especially incensed. Each in turn spoke to Grady about it.

Only Grady, John Gurney and Rosie attempted to make any reasonable excuse for Mal's actions. In spite of his concern in the matter, Grady could scarcely bring himself to talk with Mal about it.

Mal himself was oblivious to any attitudes favorable or otherwise on the part of his neighbors toward himself. He was so much taken up with the new life he was creating for himself and his insatiable desire to forget all of the past that he gave almost no thought to anything outside his immediate surroundings and possessions.

He visited with Hiram now and then on the occasions when he hired Hiram to help with jobs. He also visited with Grady when they met for meals at Mrs. Morgan's boarding house. But much to Grady's chagrin and puzzlement, Mal didn't invite him to visit in his home. It was rather disappointing to Grady, too sensitive as he was to drop in uninvited.

Rosie many times sent word by Hiram "inviting Mr. Smith to come and eat supper with us." Mal never did, which angered Hiram and hurt and puzzled Rosie.

chapter 17

THE DARK SPECTER of war hovered low over Clear Springs as two of the dreaded fateful messages followed closely one upon the other.

First, a strange man knocked one rainy night upon the door of the Hillcroft cabin bearing the regrets of the war department that their son, George B. Hillcroft, had been killed in action. The Hillcrofts and their daughter, Grace, were at home.

Mandy Hillcroft had known that this was the message she might ultimately receive, but for all that she was not prepared for the shock.

The stranger, a taxi driver from Hartstown, had stood silently by while John Hillcroft took the yellow envelope and with trembling hands tore it open to read it aloud. Mandy sank into a chair and buried her face in her apron. John, his head bowed, strode quickly to stand by her chair, his hand upon her quivering shoulder. It was the tenth such message that the taxi driver had delivered since the beginning of the war. Although many improvements and modern conveniences were coming into the Ozarks there were few telephones this far from town. When the telegraph office received an emergency message, a taxi driver was called upon to make the delivery.

There was nothing about his job that distressed this driver so much as to be selected to bear such a message to anxious loved ones. He now stood helplessly by, powerless to do anything but sympathize.

"I'm awful sorry, Ma'am," he said to Grace as she stood weeping near her parents. "If there is anything I can do—"

"Thank you, sir, you've been awfully kind. I don't know of anything you can do for us. Perhaps I should pay you for making the trip."

"The war department will take care of that," the miserable man replied, "I wish there was some way to help, but if not, I'll be going. Goodnight."

John and Mandy thanked the message bearer and said goodnight to him.

This particular driver made it a practice to stop at the home of a near neighbor of the grief-stricken family and tell them about the message he had just delivered. In this case, the house he chose was Hiram Jackson's.

Hiram and Rosie left their supper growing cold on the table while they went to take what comfort they could to Mandy and John. Hiram left Rosie with them while he went to get Grady Rogers.

Meanwhile Mrs. Morgan came puffing to her door, lantern in hand. She had heard the strange auto pass her door in the early darkness and just knew it had stopped at the Hillcrofts. It would not have had time to go farther than that.

When the car returned she was in the road to hail the driver to see if anything was wrong at Mandy's.

She was genuinely shocked and saddened at the news and came through the rain to tell the parents of her concern. Near midnight, Hiram took Mrs. Morgan back home in his truck and then returned to the Hillcroft cabin where he, Rosie and Grady Rogers sat the night through with their sorrowing neighbors.

By the end of the second day nearly every neighbor and acquaintance within five miles had heard of George's death and had called upon the family — except Mal Smith. Grady Rogers, who had been at the home almost constantly, noticed that Mal had not been near. When Hiram Jackson mentioned Mal's absence in a disdainful tone, Grady decided to make a trip to see Mal.

It was almost dark by the time Grady walked across the field to the cabin and seeing no light shining through the windows, he decided Mal must be in his newly-built barn. He found him there cleaning up his tractor.

"Glad to see you," Mal called when he saw Grady. "Excuse me here while I finish and we'll go to the house."

"Go right ahead," Grady answered cheerfully. "I haven't seen you around lately."

"No, I've been keeping busy. There's a lot of work for one man to do on a place like this."

Mal, in fact, had only been off his place long enough to eat his evening meal for the last ten days. He received no mail, newspapers or magazines so it was not necessary for him to make trips to the post office. When he did go to Hartstown or Clear Springs he always purchased enough groceries and supplies to last for two to three weeks. He was not interested in any news of the world nor the conversations and opinions of men. As long as he could remain self-sufficient, he really had neither excuse nor inclination to leave his own premises. Since he had so completely withdrawn himself few bothered to inquire about him or to seek him out.

Grady stood patiently by while Mal finished his task. Then the two friends walked toward the house.

Mal was cordial and seemed quite glad to see Grady. When they reached the kitchen door he invited Grady in. Grady exclaimed over the comfortable way he had his living quarters arranged. Then he invited Mal to walk over to Mrs. Morgan's for supper with him.

"I've been missing having supper with you," Mal said as they went along together. "Have you been away?"

Grady explained that he had been in another community for more than two weeks holding church services each evening.

"And do the people there take care of you?" Mal asked.

Grady replied that he walked home each night after the services since it was only ten miles away. Then too, someone usually came for him in the early afternoon and took him to their home for the evening meal before they went to the church. "That way I get a chance to visit in nearly every home in the community where I'm preaching," Grady went on.

"I can see where that would be helpful," his companion replied. Mal was always vaguely polite, but never seemed to take any real interest in anything that was being said. Grady made a mental note of that fact. *He seems to be drawing farther away from people and surroundings and more within himself than when he first came here,* Grady thought. *I guess I haven't been much help to him.*

Aloud he said, "I closed my work there three days ago and have been spending most of the time since then at John Hillcroft's."

"Oh, yes," Mal replied. "I heard they had received word that a son had been killed. I'm sorry indeed." He still revealed only mere politeness, as natural and detached a thing to a man of his breeding as the drawing of his breath.

So you knew of this sorrow in the home of your nearest neighbor and haven't cared enough or had interest enough to stop your work for just the length of time it would take to walk across the field and say a kind word, Grady thought as they continued together.

They reached Mrs. Morgan's boarding house after all the others had eaten. Mrs. Morgan was so out of patience and had so spent her emotions grieving with her friends, the Hillcrofts, that she set the food before the two men silently and retreated to the kitchen while they ate.

Grady, too, was somewhat out of patience. Mal had muffed every opportunity to fit into the life of the community where he had chosen to live. And apparently he was unconcerned. But Grady knew that there comes a time in every man's life when he needs friends. He wondered who besides himself would befriend Mal, who deliberately drove people away.

The folks in the valley might under some circumstances overlook Mal's "peculiar ways" but they would not forgive this evidence of indifference. Grady pondered these things in his mind and was silent during the meal as he strove to frame fitting words of rebuke to Mal.

He found that it was not easy to bring himself even to attempt to penetrate the cloak of reticence that enshrouded his strange friend. *Undoubtedly he has his reason for remaining aloof,* Grady argued to himself. *He is so dignified and leaves scarcely an opening for a rebuke. I guess the worst that could be said about him is that he withdraws from all people and lives strictly unto himself, for what reason I don't know. But certainly he has a right to live that way if he chooses.*

Still Grady was troubled. He wished Mal would not go on antagonizing his neighbors, whether deliberately or otherwise.

The two men parted at Mrs. Morgan's gate,

Mal to return to his cabin, Grady to go to the Hillcroft home. Grady had hoped that perhaps Mal would accompany him but he was doomed to disappointment for Mal did no such thing.

When Grady reached the Hillcroft home, he discovered that Mandy was composed enough to go to bed and was resting peacefully. Grace, who had the courage and strength to carry on for the sake of both her parents, was reading by the lamp. John Hillcroft was sitting in the kitchen by the cookstove talking quietly with a brother and several neighborhood friends.

John told Grady that they would like a memorial service for George held soon. It might be years before his body could be returned for a regular funeral. John asked Grady to make all of the arrangements but declared that they would not set the date until they heard from one of their boys who was still in training in the United States. They hoped that he could get a furlough and be home for the memorial service.

Grady went back to his own home to sleep that night tired in body and weary in his soul. His mind was full of the burdens of his friends, but more than anyone else he thought about Mal. Mal needed someone to penetrate the hard shell of reserve he had built around his real self to find out what kind of person he really was.

Maybe tomorrow I can think of just the right way to reach him, Grady thought as he drifted off to sleep. But the morrow brought so much more sadness to the community that Grady had no time to give any thought to Mal Smith.

Grady had slept late and was eating his breakfast about the middle of the morning when someone knocked on his door. He opened it to admit Hiram Jackson who stood before him pale and shaken. "It's our boy, Brother Rogers," Hiram said abruptly. "Word just came that he has been seriously wounded. Rosie sent me for you."

"I know there's not much you can do, Brother Rogers," Rosie greeted him as he came into the house with Hiram. "There ain't much any of us can do except pray."

"That's enough, Rosie," Grady said gently. "You have courage and you have faith. You still can hope and pray for your boy's safe return."

"I know it, Brother Rogers. And I keep thinking about Mandy and John. They know that George will never come back. It's awful hard for them."

"They are becoming reconciled," Grady returned. "That is the hardest part for any of us, I think. It is hard to say to God 'Thy will be done' and really mean it."

"You sure are right, Brother Rogers," Hiram said. "But it don't seem like it ought to be the will of God that boys like George and Frankie should be killed like that."

"Our boy has not been killed, Hiram," Rosie objected. "As long as I don't know for sure he is dead I'm going to keep praying he will get all right again."

"Perhaps it isn't God's will that these boys should die, Hiram," Grady explained patiently, "but I'm convinced that it is His will that a person shall accept whatever adversity comes in his life without bitterness and with the faith that all things work together for good."

"It sure is good to have you here, Brother Rogers," Rosie said. "We need someone like you to help us to hold on to our faith."

While Grady sat talking with his anxious friends, Mandy and John Hillcroft came. They had heard of Frankie's wounds and put aside their own deep sorrow to bring comfort to these younger parents who had but one son to lose.

Many friends and neighbors came to the Jackson cabin within the next week to add their prayers and hopes for Frankie's complete recovery, but Mal Smith was not among them. Grady Rogers felt more puzzled than ever and deeply concerned for Mal.

chapter 18

ALTHOUGH MAL had made arrangements
with the Goodmans to buy a quart of milk each day,
he became so engrossed in his work that he sometimes let a day or so go by without making the necessary trip to obtain it.

One time almost a week elapsed in which
he did without milk. These were the days when
he was building a new barn and was so anxious to
get the job finished that he began hammering as
soon as it was light enough to see the nails and did
not cease as long as the light lasted. Mal was not
conditioned for such arduous labor and had no
energy left at the end of the day for doing extra
chores. So instead of making the trip over the hill
for a quart of milk he was contented to drop his
exhausted body into bed to recuperate for the
next day's demand on his physical strength.

Ann Goodman did not like the days when
Mal Smith failed to come for his quart of milk.
True, Mal did not show much friendliness on the
days when he did come. He never even took the
time or trouble to sit down for a cup of coffee or a
piece of pie although Ann or Mrs. Goodman usually
invited him to do so. Usually Mal just stood on
the porch or in the kitchen and waited. So when
it happened that days had gone by and Mal

had failed to appear, Ann decided to be neighborly
and take a supply of milk to him. Although the
crisp frosty nights of early November had arrived,
the days were still bright and sunny. Ann had
listened to the pounding of the hammers and knew
that work ceased during the noon hour so she decided if she expected to see Mal she had better
be on hand when he was not busy.

One day when he went to the house for
lunch there she was sitting in the sun upon his
doorstep.

"I've brought you milk, butter and eggs,"
she called gaily. "No doubt you would work until
you starved if somone didn't look after you."

"I certainly do thank you," Mal replied
worriedly. "But you surely shouldn't have done it."

"Why not?" Mal wondered why Ann must
always seem so openly defiant — and so provocative
too, he might have added. She most assuredly was
an extremely attractive woman but he had not the
slightest intention of being ensnared by her charm.

"You should know why not," he said sternly.
"I live alone here and can scarcely be expected to
entertain ladies. Besides, you can't know if it is
even safe to come here. I am a stranger, after all."

"How can I know if it is safe unless I make
some effort to find out?" Ann retorted daringly.
"And besides you don't need to stay a stranger forever. Why don't you give folks a chance to know
you?"

"I keep myself a stranger, because I like it

that way," Mal rebuffed. He was really quite angry with Ann and her boldness. "And it will not be necessary for you to repeat this touching, neighborly act. I plan to buy a cow as soon as I have a shelter completed for one."

"There'll be other things you will need," Ann drawled unruffled. Mal could not fail to notice the tantalizing challenge in her eyes. "And thanks for everything."

"Same to you," Mal retorted, grinning at her roguish upturned face in spite of himself.

"Women," Mal muttered savagely as he stomped into the cabin after Ann was gone — beautiful ones, ugly ones, or merely the indifferent type like Mary Goodman. He wanted nothing to do with them.

Hiram, who had helped Mal with much of the building, was already at work when Mal finished his lunch and returned to the unfinished barn that day. The older man had such a dark and forbidding look upon his face that Mal kept silent. Ann Goodman, strolling lazily through the woods in the afternoon sun, smiled to herself as she listened to the far away pounding. She was sure she detected a certain viciousness in the steady thud-thud of the hammers. She thought she knew why Mal was angry with her.

As the two men left off work late that afternoon, Mal asked Hiram if he knew who might have a good milk cow for sale.

"Sure do now, Mal," Hiram replied. "John

Hillcroft's got a plumb good cow to sell. He was tellin' me just the other day that he didn't believe he could winter all his stuff. Said he'd sell a good cow."

"Thanks," Mal answered. "I'll go over in the morning to see him. I can put her in the part of the barn that is finished."

Mal had worked furiously that afternoon, but somehow did not feel the customary satisfaction from his self-imposed routine of hard labor. After he had prepared and eaten a bountiful supper, he noticed a bit of chilliness in the house.

Good time to build a fire in the fireplace, he decided. When the flames were crackling cheerily, he sprawled in the great chair to watch the jagged tongues of fire leap into the air toward the opening of the great blackened chimney. But he was not in a good mood for dreaming nor for drowsiness. Rather he was seized by a disturbing restlessness. Soon he had forgotten the fire and was wandering about the room trying first one activity and then another to relieve the restless anxiety that possessed him. He moved to the piano and selected several pieces to play but none of them seemed to fit his mood. Then he selected a book by a favorite author but could scarcely sit still long enough to finish one chapter.

He wandered into the kitchen, built a fire, washed the supper dishes and made a pot of coffee which he did not drink.

"Well," he said to himself when every chore

he could think of had been done, "I guess this is the time to get started on those book shelves." He searched until he found the measuring tape and worked until he had the dimensions of all the lumber he would need and planned mentally to go the next day to Hartstown to buy the needed materials.

It was two A.M. when Mal finally tumbled into bed. As he drifted into sleep the picture of a pretty young woman sitting on his door-step shimmered in his mind.

The next morning Mal drove past John Hillcroft's place on his way to Hartstown and stopped to see about buying the cow.

"'Bout time you was a comin' over for a visit," his neighbor greeted him. "I been a lookin' for you."

"I've been terribly busy," Mal replied. "I'm trying to get a new barn built before winter comes."

"Yes, I been a hearin' the hammerin'. Hiram's a helpin' you, ain't he?"

Mal did not want to waste time talking. He was anxious to get to Hartstown and back before noon. The sky was growing hazy to the north and he feared the good weather might not last much longer.

"Yes, Hiram's helping me," he answered, "and he told me you had a cow to sell."

"I sure have," John Hillcroft said, "a plumb good one, too. Gives about three gallons to the milkin'. How big a barn you buildin'? I been aimin' to get over there ever' day, but ain't got around to it yet. Had to get up all my winter wood by myself."

"Where is the cow you have to sell?" Mal interrupted him, wondering how long John would talk if some one didn't stop him.

"Just turned her in the pasture. Did you want to see her?"

"Yes, if it's not too much trouble." Mal tried not to reveal his impatience.

"Ain't ary bit of trouble," his host assured him as Mal followed him through a series of gates to the open pasture. John singled out a good cow and calf, too. "What do you think of her?"

"She looks good to me," Mal answered. "Of course, one can't tell much about her milk giving capacity so soon after she's had her calf."

"Why don't you happen around about milkin' time this evening?" Hillcroft suggested. "Then you can tell more about the kind of cow she is. Can milk her if you want."

"I doubt if I'd have time today," Mal answered. "I have quite a lot of work planned. But I could come over in the morning."

"Tomorrow is Sunday. Reckon you livin' over there by yourself you plumb forget the days of the week."

Mal opened his mouth to say that he had not forgotten, then thought better of it.

Instead he said, "All right, Mr. Hillcroft. I'll

come over late this afternoon, before you milk." Then he asked about the price of the cow.

"Well, now the price with the calf would be one thing and without it 'twould be another," John Hillcroft said deliberately.

Mal thought he would want the calf and said so. "I don't know how I could use all of that milk," he elaborated.

"The thing to do would be to buy another calf the same age as this one and put both of them on the cow."

Mal had wondered if this would be practical, but had hesitated to ask. Before he had a chance to make a comment his neighbor added, "I have another young calf just a week older than this one that I'm trying to wean from its mother. I'd sell you both of them and they'd take about all the milk this cow would give."

They went together to the barn to see the other calf and John quoted Mal some prices. At length, Mal said he would return that afternoon and if he liked the looks of the cow then he would buy her and the calves.

chapter 19

SHORTLY AFTER GEORGE HILLCROFT's memorial service Thanksgiving came to the Ozarks. According to a long-standing custom the people of Clear Springs planned to gather at the schoolhouse for a turkey dinner and worship service. Grady Rogers had conducted these services for many years. He always depended on Rosie Jackson and her family, the John Hillcrofts and Mary Goodman to help him with the music and details of the meeting.

There was almost never any work planned for the day and about the only families who failed to attend were those who left the valley to visit relatives in the more remote places.

Grady made a special trip on the evening before Thanksgiving Day to see his neighbor Mal Smith and ask him to the schoolhouse for Thanksgiving festivities. Much to his surprise Mal accepted the invitation.

Mal admitted that he had already had an invitation to partake in the holiday. Rosie had sent a delicious freshly baked pumpkin pie by Hiram that afternoon asking him to be ready to go with them to the schoolhouse on the next day for Thanksgiving turkey.

"The spicy flavor of the pie made me remember the Thanksgivings when I was a boy on my

grandfather's farm," Mal explained. "My grand-
mother was a wonderful cook—always seemed to
know just what small boys liked best. I'll really
enjoy a turkey dinner, cranberry sauce and pumpkin
pie once more. So I told Hiram to tell Rosie I'd
like to go."

"You'll be glad you went," Grady replied.
"These Ozark women can really cook! And you'll
enjoy the fellowship too. I don't mean to be critical
but I'm afraid you've kept too much to yourself
since coming here. That's seldom good for a man,"
Grady spoke gently.

Mal Smith had lapsed into a deep study.
He and his visitor sat in the deep lounging chairs
that flanked the huge fireplace where a cozy fire
crackled.

When Mal did not speak, Grady wondered
if he had been too blunt. He certainly had no desire to offend.

Finally Mal stirred and shifted his position.
He turned and looked into Grady's face for a brief
moment. Then he turned once more and gazing
into the fire's blaze he remarked, "The war did a
lot of things to a lot of people."

Grady, scarcely ever at a loss for words,
hardly knew how to carry on the conversation from
there. Mal's words might have been a rebuke
except for the detached way in which he spoke.
Nevertheless, Grady felt slightly embarrassed and
rose to take his leave.

"Don't hurry away," Mal invited. "If you

have time I have something on my mind that I'd like to talk to you about."

"I have plenty of time," Grady answered and resuming his seat he waited expectantly.

"I have been working here on my farm for several months now," Mal began, "testing soil and studying conditions with a view to deciding the best paying crops. I'm convinced that the best money-makers are dairying and strawberries. The only drawback to investing in these crops is the serious shortage of markets for these products."

"But if the farmers in this section would get together and organize for cooperative marketing that handicap would be eliminated," Grady suggested.

"Exactly. The question is — are they progressive enough in their thinking to adopt such a plan?" Mal wanted to know.

Grady had witnessed many changes and advances in the lives and living of these citizens of the valley during the more than twenty years he had dwelt there. He was quick to spring to their defense.

"Once the hillman understands that a thing is for his permanent good economically, spiritually or socially, he is as eager to make use of it as anyone," the preacher explained. "And I'm sure if he understands the advantages of cooperative marketing he'll accept it readily."

"And where would that understanding begin?"

"My suggestion, Mal, would be to call the

farmers in this section together and let someone who has the ability explain the subject and the advantages."

"I'm a man of action," Mal said. "When can the meeting be called and what is the best way to get word to the right people?"

"Next Friday night will be a good date," Grady said. "The announcement can be made tomorrow."

"Fine," said Mal. "You make the announcement and I'll prepare to talk to them about co-operative marketing."

Thanksgiving Day dawned crisp and cool after a heavy frost during the night. By noon when the folk were gathering for the festivities, however, the sun had warmed the land and clothed the hills with brightness.

The women spread the dinner while the men gathered in small groups in the bright sunshine for conversation. Mal came into the schoolyard unaccompanied. While several persons noticed him, no one made a move to invite him into the circles of neighbors and friends.

Grady Rogers, however, had been on the lookout for Mal. When he saw him come into the yard he moved quickly toward him and piloted him toward the schoolhouse. He knew he could depend upon the natural friendliness of Rosie and Mary Goodman to help make Mal feel welcome.

Rosie and Mary were shy but gracious with him. They were aware, as was everyone else, that

Mal was quite different from the men of the valley.

When the men were finally called to dinner, Rosie supplied Mal with table utensils. The teacher of the school, Grace Hillcroft, rapped loudly upon her desk for order and when the room was quiet she asked Grady Rogers to "return thanks." Grady's prayer included an expression of gratitude for the blessings of life and a simple petition for sufficient grace in their lives to enable them as a group of Christians to live in accordance with God's purposes.

At the conclusion of the prayer, plate in hand, the men and children fell into a single line on each side of the table heaping their plates full with their choice from the dishes set before them.

Grady found a place for Mal in the line beside him. Grady heaped his plate high from many dishes while Mal served himself sparingly from only a few.

Too bad, Grady thought. *If he could only eat heartily from many dishes then he could honestly compliment the ladies on their cooking. That's one of the best ways into the hearts of these people.*

When all had finished eating and the dishes were cleared away, the worship service began. Ann Goodman was called upon to play the piano and John Hillcroft led the singing with his fine baritone. To Mal, who failed to note the spirit and heartiness with which the people sang, the music sounded crude and faulty.

No part of the program impressed him except Ann's excellent performance at the piano. Her playing was far from spiritual but was nevertheless skillful. Unmistakably the girl possessed rare talent. While Grady spoke Mal listened attentively and wished devoutly that he still believed in the things about which Grady talked.

Before the audience was dismissed Rosie Jackson asked if she might make an announcement. When given the floor she expressed her grave concern for the safety of her son. She asked their friends who could to remain after the meeting to pray for him.

Grady Rogers asked John Hillcroft to pronounce the benediction after which a few young men left the building. Ann also rose to go and whispered to Mal that he would not to expected to stay. Mal had no inclination to stay any longer but did not know how he could escape. He eagerly welcomed Ann's invitation to depart.

Once outside he fell in step beside the aggressive young woman and they strolled off together along the wooded path that lead toward Ann's home. When they reached her door, Mal followed her into the house. Soon he found himself seated at the piano playing as he had not played in years while Ann sang in her clear contralto or listened with a look of enraptured appreciation on her face.

Two hours later, when Mary and Mrs. Goodman came home, it was nearly dark. Mal could not believe that the afternoon had slipped so quickly away.

Explaining that he must hurry home to do his evening chores, he refused an invitation to stay for supper. He bid them a curt goodbye and took his departure, carrying with him a feeling of anger and resentment against Ann which he did not take the trouble to analyze.

Mal walked as fast as he could to reach home. He wanted to run away from something, he knew not what. The afternoon had been pleasant but still he was displeased with himself. He vowed that he would not permit himself to be persuaded again to depart from the rigid routine of life he had set up for himself. He put the whole matter from his mind and refused to review the events of the day.

He dawdled with his chores as long as he could and then prepared his evening meal. He occupied the rest of the evening with preparations for the talk he planned to present on cooperative marketing.

chapter 20

WHEN MAL arrived on the night appointed for the meeting, Stony Point School was well filled. Two score or more hill farmers grouped near the open door were discussing strawberry culture pro and con. Most of them thought such gardening was for women and "young'uns" as they put it.

Mal spoke to the men as he walked in. He chose a seat near the front just back of the women grouped together in the front seats and the long bench along the side wall.

Grady Rogers stood behind the teacher's desk, which was also used as a pulpit on Sundays. John Hillcroft and several other men who were community leaders were conversing earnestly with him.

Picking up the hand bell used to call the children from their play to the study sessions, Grady handed it to a teen-aged girl.

"Ring the bell, Carol, and call the men in," he requested.

Conversations slowly ceased as the men filed in to stand along the walls. The large crowd in attendance had already taken all the available seats. Among those who entered were four or five young men carrying guitars, fiddles and other musical instruments. Ann was already seated at the piano.

What goes on here? Mal thought to himself. *Must these people constantly be strumming on guitar strings?* This was a meeting for discussing business. He could not see that there was any need for playing and singing. He felt himself growing irritated.

Grady had quite purposely invited the musicians to be present, however. In the first place, he knew, nothing could put these folks in a good mood as quickly as an hour of playing and singing favorite tunes. Then, too, he thought that if the meeting did not go as well as he and Mal hoped, the music would furnish a happy relief from any tension that might develop. He knew that these people did not feel friendly toward Mal and he was not sure that they would accept his suggestions. They might even interpret the whole matter as plain interference.

When everyone had found a place for himself, Grady asked them to sing an opening verse of "America." Ann's clear voice could be heard above all the rest, exactly as she intended.

When the song ended Grady stepped forward and said, "Let us pray." His voice rang with sincerity and faith as he asked God's blessing and guidance in the meeting. An earnest appeal for God's watchful care for the ill or distressed ended the prayer. Grady then briefly explained the purpose of the gathering, asking if anyone had anything to say before he called on Mal Smith to explain the prospects and possibilities of strawberry culture in the Ozarks. No one spoke and Grady turned the meeting over to Mal.

"Let me say in the beginning I am not here in the role of a public speaker," Mal began. "I just want to tell you the little I know about this matter as quickly as I can. Then we'll make it very informal, you asking any questions you are interested in. We'll discuss the questions together and try to arrive at an answer . . ."

Mal then explained how well suited the land thereabouts was to grazing and strawberry raising, pointing out how strawberries should be planted.

"But what about getting the berries to the market?" someone asked. "I thought that was what we come here to hear about."

"I'm coming to that," Mal replied. If he detected any animosity in his inquirer's manner he did not reveal it.

"The wholesale house in Springfield will sign a contract with any association to take the berries at top price. We will have to deliver them to the highway. That means we will probably have to build a shed on the highway for housing."

"We are more than twelve miles from the highway," Grady remarked. "It would be necessary to have some kind of transportation to carry the crates of berries to the loading shed."

"My truck is a ton and a half capacity. It would be available. Perhaps there are other trucks, too, that could be used," Mal answered.

At the conclusion of Mal's talk no other

questions were and asked and Grady knew from the
sullen looks on several faces that further efforts at
discussing the matter would be futile. He had
hoped that perhaps an association could be formed.
He had worked with these people for many years,
however, and he knew they either accepted an idea
wholeheartedly or rejected it altogether. So, much
to Mal's dismay, the preacher brought the meeting
to an abrupt close and set the music makers to
playing.

The people gathered there soon forgot Mal
and were having a good time talking, laughing and
singing. Various persons were called upon to sing
a special song and no one refused.

Later during the evening Ann turned from
her place at the piano and suggested to Grady
Rogers that Mr. Smith was good at the piano.
"Why not ask him to play?" Mal could cheerfully
have wrung her neck, but he did not fail to note
the taunt in her tone and the mocking smile on her
face. There was nothing for him to do but comply.
He strode stiffly to the piano wishing with all of
his might that he could once and for all put this
impertinent young woman in her place.

When Mal was angry he invariably chose
to play selections from Chopin. That, of course,
was unfortunate in this unsophisticated gathering.
No one understood the music, but everyone seemed
to sense Mal's anger, especially his tormenter. She
was amused and greatly pleased with herself.

Rosie knew something was amiss in the performance but couldn't decide what. Both Grady and Mary shared a feeling of impatience with Ann for putting Mal at her mercy. They both knew Ann to be ruthless. They knew that she was punishing Mal because she had not been able to break through his reserve.

Scowls of distrust clouded the faces of Mal's listeners. When he finished playing only the few who felt they must be polite applauded him.

Instead of returning to his former seat Mal moved from the piano to the back of the room and waited for an opportunity to leave without attracting attention.

The next day when Grady and Mal met at Mrs. Morgan's Mal asked why they had failed to organize a Cooperative Strawberry Association.

"It wasn't that those farmers were not convinced that cooperative marketing was to their advantage. It was something else. They seemed to resent me. Why?" Mal wanted to know.

"You've asked me, Mal, and I'm going to give it to you straight," Grady replied.

"That's the way I want it," Mal replied.

"Well," Grady almost stammered as he hesitated momentarily. "Your attitude since coming here to live has not been pleasing to the folk who live here."

"What do you mean by my attitude?" Mal asked. "I mind my own business. I pay good wages for help and I haven't asked any favors."

"But you haven't put yourself out to be very friendly, have you?"

"I didn't come here to make friends," Mal responded. "I came here to find a place where I could be left alone and could find an independent way to make a living."

Grady smiled, "And haven't you been left alone?" he asked kindly.

"Yes."

"But are you very sure you want complete independence? If so, why did you try to interest these folk in cooperative marketing?"

"Cooperative farming would be advantageous to them," Mal defended.

"Certainly it would," Grady agreed, "but before you can sell any new idea to them, you need to gain their confidence."

"What do you think I should do?"

"The answer is simple. Become interested in their affairs," Grady advised.

"But I have no interest in their affairs," Mal objected.

"Mal," Grady said directly, "who are your friends?"

"I have no friends."

"But a man needs friends. He can't be happy without someone to take an interest in him — someone to care."

"Happiness is not important," Mal insisted. "Only peace and independence matter. Happiness never lasts."

"I don't agree, Mal. Happiness is the one important thing in life. Without it life would scarcely be worthwhile."

"That is scarcely the logic I should have expected from you," Mal answered. "I should have thought you would list honesty, loyalty, hard work and charity to be more important than happiness."

"As I see it those are the things from which happiness is made. Add to it service to God and man and friendliness and you have all things needed for happiness."

"What about faith?" Mal argued. "Can happiness be found without faith?"

"That depends upon where you place your faith," Grady replied. "Faith placed in God and goodness and your fellowman accompanies happiness while a misplaced trust in one's self or in wealth or power or in long hours of hard work results only in frustration and discontent."

Grady recalled that Mal had made this same inquiry on the day they had gone fishing together soon after Mal came to Clear Springs.

"Mal," Grady said kindly, "I do not know what has happened to you to destroy your faith. Perhaps your experience in the war. I do not know. But I do know you must learn to trust again. You need to re-establish a faith in things good and worthwhile and eternal."

"But how, Grady? How?" Once again Mal Smith revealed the anguish of his tortured soul.

"A good place to start is in the community

where you have chosen to live," Grady advised. "Try to get acquainted with your neighbors. You are a man of culture, education and good breeding. These folk of this valley live with honesty, sincerity of purpose and simplicity. Surely your interests are not entirely incompatible?"

The two men had sat talking at the table for more than an hour. Now Mrs. Morgan began fussing about the room and Grady knew she was anxious to clear the table. With a pleasant remark to her, he arose and Mal followed him. They parted at the front gate, Mal to stroll alone through the woods to his home to do the chores, Grady to visit a sick neighbor.

When Mal came within sight of his house, he noticed a light was in his cabin. *Must be Hiram and perhaps even Rosie,* he thought with a strange gladness in his heart. Maybe Grady Rogers had been right. Perhaps if he was going to make his home here it would be better to try to establish friendly relations with the folk here. He believed he was more attracted to Hiram than anyone else. Aside from Grady, of course. But he was not a mountaineer, though he was much like them.

Perhaps it is something he has acquired through the years he has lived here, thought Mal, *but more than likely it is because he naturally enjoys a life of honest and simple living.*

Mal entered his house through the back door, strode through the kitchen to the living room where he was greeted not by Hiram or Rosie but by Ann Goodman. She had lighted the wood in the fireplace and made an adorable picture curled contentedly in a nearby easy chair.

Even Mal's surprise and anger did not blind him to her loveliness. Ann detected this and felt triumphant.

"Surprised?" she asked archly.

"Surprised and annoyed with you, Ann," Mal said sternly. "I remember telling you once you shouldn't come here alone."

"I'm convinced you are a gentleman. Why should I be afraid to come here alone?"

"You certainly have no reason whatsoever to be afraid of me," Mal said icily. "But perhaps you should remember that it isn't quite the proper thing to do."

"I've tried being proper at different times in my life and always found it horribly dull," Ann was being deliberately provocative. Mal suddenly determined not to allow her presence to disturb him.

"Will you excuse me, please, while I do the milking and the other chores?" he inquired politely.

Ann assured him she would be quite happy during his absence. Before he returned to the house she had made a plate of fudge and a pot of coffee. On a small table before the fire were pieces of the banana cream pie she had brought with her. The table was all set when Mal returned to the house.

When Mal returned he seemed to have forgotten completely his earlier irritation and conversed gaily with Ann. He praised the coffee and pie and made some inane remark that a man didn't get along very adequately without a woman in the home. Ann accepted the compliments with a grace and charm that she considered to be just right for the occasion and failed to volunteer the information that the pie was one of several that had been baked by her sister Mary that afternoon.

For an hour following the repast Mal played the piano while Ann sang. Then Mal suggested that he take the walk with her through the moonlit woods to her home.

Returning to his cabin alone later in the evening Mal reflected upon the pleasant evening. A feeling of loneliness overcame him when he entered his room and breathed into his nostrils the faint lingering breath of a woman's perfume. Mal sat in a deep chair before the blazing fire and dozed. For some reason his usual dream of Kathy was not clear, but was confused with a face that seemed to be Kathy's but instead of being framed with black curls it was surrounded by red hair that shone like burnished copper.

chapter **21**

THE NEXT DAY was a cold, drizzly Sunday and Mal awoke tired and depressed. His rest had been broken by several hours of wakefulness while his brain whirled with thoughts of Ann Goodman and his other neighbors.

Mal did not want the hostility of his neighbors to disturb his peace of mind. But he lacked the power to keep thoughts of the situation from occupying much of his thinking.

He wondered how much of Grady Rogers' conclusions about his position in the community were justified. He entertained a certain resentment against Grady for some of the things he had said. Yet he had to admit the man had given him an honest answer to his inquiry.

Mal stood gazing out through the large window in his living room. A steady rain was falling. He hated days like this. He wanted to be in the fields blotting out bitter memories with long hours of toil.

He supposed it would be best for him to go to church. Certainly Rosie, Hiram, Grady and others had invited him often enough. Then too, Grady Rogers was a capable speaker and minister of the Word. But an unaccountable stubbornness restrained him.

188

He had been planning to build a pen on one side of the barn so that the cows could come in and out as they pleased. Although the rain continued to fall Mal decided to go ahead and build the cow lot immediately. *The rain in my face will be more tolerable than having to stay inside and listen to it beat on the roof,* he thought as he donned a waterproof jacket and went toward the barn.

He set at once to digging post holes spaced twelve feet apart. The plans called for boards twelve feet long to be nailed to the posts. Mal had had the lumber sawed from oak trees carefully selected in his woods and stored away for future use. He also used his own timber for the posts. He and Hiram had made them when they repaired his fences.

Placing the posts in the holes, he pounded clay and rock around them with an iron crow bar. By midafternoon the fence was finished. The rain was now only a slow drizzle, but the sun had failed to break through the gray clouds. The damp air was cool.

Mal would have returned at once to the house to cook his delayed noon meal, but he glanced up and noticed a long two by four nailed to the roof of the barn. John Hillcroft had placed it there to brace himself when he shingled the roof of the barn. *That isn't good for the roof,* Mal thought as his gaze rested upon it. *It'll hold water from running off the roof — eventually it'll cause some rotting for sure. John should have removed it. I'll do it now.*

Fitting his words to action, Mal carried his ladder from the barn and climbed to the roof, a long prying bar in hand. Standing near the top of the ladder, Mal reached up and inserted the bar under the long obstruction on the roof. Prying with the rod he loosened the board wherever it was nailed down. Toward the end of the two by four the reach proved to be too far and Mal slipped just as he succeeded in loosening it. Managing to secure a hold on the roof's edge, he hung there. At the same instant the heavy board broke loose from its hold and slid down the steep wet roof. It struck Mal on the head and he fell with the heavy ladder. With a thud he landed on a pile of rock that had been left from building the foundation of the barn. There he lay still and unconscious in the cold rain.

Grady Rogers had gone home with Hiram and Rosie Jackson from church that morning to eat the noon meal with them and visit through the afternoon. The Jacksons were still anxiously awaiting further word about their wounded son. Rosie had never ceased to pray for his safe return and had besought her friends to continue praying. It gave her great comfort to have Grady Rogers visit and pray with them.

It was customary for Grady to hold services on Sunday evening also. Because of the heavy rain that had fallen during the night and even up to the

morning worship hour, he knew the streams sur-
rounding the schoolhouse would be overflowing,
making it dangerous if not impossible for the hill
people to come out. Therefore, he announced that
there would be no preaching service that night.

After an enjoyable afternoon with the Jackson family, he took his departure about five o'clock
telling Rosie he expected to stop on his way home
to visit a little with Mal Smith.

"It'll be a good thing for him," Rosie said.
"I can't help thinking a lot about him being over
there by himself so much. Especially on a day like
this."

"I reckon that's the way he likes it," Hiram
said grumpily. "He didn't seem to want no friends."

Grady was glad that Hiram had not heard
Mal declare a few days before that he had no need
for friends. He kept hoping that he could discover
a way to help Mal change his attitude before his
chance of ever being accepted in the community
disappeared.

It was nearly dark when Grady reached
Mal's. Finding no light in the house he went at
once to the barn where he expected to find Mal
milking. Not finding Mal in the barn he started to
circle the building. That was when he stumbled
onto the unconscious form. It was the work of a
moment to lift the helpless body down from the
rock pile. Then raising Mal to a half-sitting position, Grady slipped his arms from the back under
Mal's arms and across his chest. Carefully he

pulled the inert body into the barn out of the chilling rain.

Then he ran quickly to the house for blankets. Back at the barn he covered the still unconscious Mal and hurried back to Jackson's for help.

Hiram and Rosie both returned with him in their truck. The men worked rapidly to fashion a litter and carried Mal to the house. Rosie built fires to warm the house and made a pot of steaming coffee.

The men stripped Mal's water soaked clothes from him and redressed him in pajamas and a heavy dressing robe which they found hanging in the clothes closet.

Grady thought it best not to lose time trying to get a doctor. "We'd better take him right in to the hospital at Springfield," he directed. "Open a bale of hay and spread it out on the truck bed. Cover it with a blanket. Then tie the tarpauline tight over the rack on the truck. That will keep the wind out. I don't know how badly he is hurt—broken leg for one thing. The bone is projecting through the skin. Also a head injury—probably concussion. But his greatest danger is pneumonia."

Rosie went to help Hiram prepare the truck while Grady stayed with the patient. He regained consciousness at intervals and Grady seized such opportunities to get as much hot coffee into him as possible.

Within an hour's time the truck was rolling

toward Springfield with Hiram at the wheel and Grady sitting in the truck bed doing what he could for the injured Mal.

It was nearly midnight when they finally drove up to the receiving entrance to the hospital.

Orderlies quickly carried the unconscious man to the emergency room. Hiram parked the truck and he and Grady sat in the waiting room until the doctor completed an examination. Then the doctor called them in to explain that Mal had a compound fracture of the right leg, a simple fracture of the left arm above the elbow and a brain concussion. Naturally, there were also symptoms of severe shock. "But his greatest danger now is pneumonia. If we can prevent that he will be okay," the doctor concluded.

Then he asked, "Are you men relatives?"

"No, just neighbors. My name is Rogers," Grady informed him. "This is Hiram Jackson. I found Mr. Smith lying unconscious in the rain. We brought him here as quickly as possible," Grady explained.

"Well, his relatives should know of his condition," the doctor replied. "He's really in a bad way."

"He lived alone. I'm not sure he has relatives. I've never heard him mention anyone. Have you, Hiram?"

"No, I never have," Hiram replied. "He never seemed to care much for folks."

"Can he pay for special nursing care?"

the doctor wanted to know. "He really should have more attention than the floor nurses can give him."

"I really do not know anything about his finances," Grady Rogers asserted. "But if he needs a nurse, by all means secure one for him. I'll be personally responsible. She'll receive her money in advance."

"Very well, Mr. Rogers," the doctor replied. "And do you plan to remain in the city until your friend is better?"

"I'll stay until he regains consciousness and can make his own plans," Grady replied.

"That's fine," the doctor said. "Please stay in the room until the nurse arrives. Then you might leave word with her where you can be reached."

The doctor took another look at Mal as he lay breathing quickly and groaning occasionally. Then he left the room. Until a nurse arrived, Grady and Hiram sat with Mal. Then Hiram took the truck and started back toward Clear Springs. Grady Rogers secured a room at the Y.M.C.A. and went to bed.

It was past ten o'clock in the morning before he awoke, dressed, had his breakfast and returned to the hospital. A different nurse was in charge in Mal's room. Grady introduced himself and explained briefly what he knew about Mal's accident. Handing her his check, he apologized to the nurse for not being on hand to pay her in advance for Mal's care.

Grady had a small amount of money put away in a Springfield bank in case of an emergency. He drew occasionally upon it for charity needs among the people with whom he labored. He was using money from that fund to pay for Mal's care.

When Grady asked about Mal's condition he was told that the patient was sleeping under a sedative but had been delirious. He had been calling over and over for "Kathy." Did Grady know who "Kathy" might be? And had the patient been in service? He kept shouting orders about bombers and missions, etc.

"Really, nurse, I don't know much about him," Grady replied. "He came to our area some time ago, but kept very much to himself. He told me on one occasion that he was a navigator on a bomber during the war and had a medical discharge."

Just then the doctor came into the room, greeted Grady and studied Mal's chart. He asked the nurse a few questions and said to Grady, "He'll remain in a state of shock for a day or so. It's those long hours of exposure in the rain. So far we have kept out pneumonia. There isn't much we can do now, but for time and treatment to do its part."

When the doctor was gone from the room, Grady sat down to watch with the nurse. Still weary, he soon dropped off to sleep. How long he slept he did not know, but was suddenly awakened when Mal sat up in bed and screamed,

"The bomber's hit! She's on fire! Jump boys! Jump! Kathy! Kathy, where are you?"

The nurse, speaking in a firm gentle voice, said, "Right here, Mal. Kathy's here. Now lie down. Everything is all right."

"Thank you, nurse," Mal said, suddenly calm. "But I'm not Mal. My name is John Smith. John Malcom Smith. Understand, nurse?"

"Yes, I understand," the nurse said quietly. "Now try to rest." Mal lay quite still and the nurse released her hold on him. She smiled across the bed at the deeply puzzled Grady Rogers. *Why had Mal insisted that his name was John?* he wondered. *And who was Kathy?* Perhaps the answers to these questions would explain Mal's reluctance to reveal anything about his life before coming to Clear Springs.

Another day passed before Mal finally regained consciousness. By that time, although his fractures had been set, pneumonia had developed. Mal was seriously ill. But by Friday the doctors pronounced him out of danger. When he knew all was well Grady went back to Clear Springs to be on hand for Sunday's services.

Everyone in the valley was deeply interested in Mal's condition. From their changed attitudes one could scarcely believe that just a week before some of the same people had severely condemned him as selfish, greedy and unfriendly.

Since Mal's accident Hiram Jackson had milked his cow and cared for his hogs. Mal had no other livestock at the barn. John Hillcroft looked after the beef cattle on pasture.

On Monday Grady returned to the hospital and found Mal much improved and able to talk. The injured man wanted to know many things but was most interested in discharging his obligations without delay. He insisted on repaying Grady for the special nurse.

"There's plenty of time for that," Grady demurred. "The thing for you to do now is get well."

But Mal insisted. Grady claimed Mal's billfold at the hospital desk and extracted enough money to pay all he had advanced. Because Mal insisted, he also paid the hospital in full for his care to date. The bills all paid, Grady returned the nearly empty billfold to him.

"I have a checking account in the Hartstown Bank," Mal explained. "I can write checks for the rest of the time I am here."

Grady did not stay long in Mal's room. The nurse had told him that the patient needed as much rest as he could get.

By the next day Mal's fever had completely left him and he was out of danger. He only needed rest, food and care. Grady returned to Clear Springs after assuring Mal that he would return in a few days.

chapter 22

A FEW DAYS LATER, when he returned to visit Mal at the hospital, Grady found him to be no better, and the doctors and nurses puzzled because there seemed to be no reason why he had not responded quickly to the treatment he was receiving. Still, Mal remained in a lethargic condition with a slight rise in temperature during his waking hours. He ate poorly and answered questions in noncommittal monosyllables.

As soon as he arrived Grady was summoned to the doctor's office for a consultation.

"There seems to be something on his mind," the doctor explained Mal's condition. "We thought perhaps you could give us some information about the man that would help."

Grady repeated that he knew almost nothing about Mal's personal life but told what he knew of Mal's coming to the valley and his reticent attitude.

"I have had a great deal of experience with men," Grady said, "and in several instances have been able to help. Something tells me that sooner or later I can help Mal."

"The man certainly needs help from someone," the doctor exclaimed.

Rising from his chair across the desk from

the doctor Grady said, "Mal needs to discover that God can help him. When he learns that everything else will be all right."

Grady again took a room at the Y.M.C.A. and spent all the time he possibly could with Mal. He brought the sick man magazines and papers. At first Mal only thanked him politely, but as the days passed he began talking and taking part in the entertainment being provided for him. Grady made the happy discovery that Mal really had a fine sense of humor and he exerted every effort to bring laughter to the hospital room. He never once relaxed his efforts to be a cheerful visitor.

Mal's health began to show a marked improvement. Then came Saturday and Grady had to go back to Clear Springs for Sunday services.

Left to his own resources, Mal again became absorbed with thoughts of himself and once more grew morose and depressed.

The doctor and nurses noted the change in his progress toward normality and were as glad to see Grady return on the following Monday as Mal was himself. Grady brought a small radio with him which he placed in Mal's room.

"Thanks a lot," Mal said politely. He did not care at all to listen to radio programs, but he was touched by Grady's kindness.

"Oh, don't thank me," Grady replied lightly. "I have been missing the radio so my motive in bringing one along was rather selfish."

Since Grady put it that way, Mal knew he

would have to listen to the radio whether he wanted to or not. He did not suspect that was Grady's real motive in bringing the radio.

Mal now began to fret because his friend was going to the expense and trouble of spending so much of his time with him. Grady had to manufacture an excuse for being in town.

"Don't worry about me, Mal," he said. "I've been wanting to do some research study on a certain subject for a long time and so this is a ready-made opportunity to make use of the public library as well as the library at the Teacher's College while I watch you get well. Really, I am the one who is being accommodated. I'm much obliged to you for breaking a few bones."

Mal smiled wryly. "I'm not convinced, Preacher," he replied, "but I suppose there is nothing I can do or say to keep you from doing more for me than a man could expect from his own brother. I only hope I can repay you someday."

"Mal, if I've been of any help, that's all that matters," Grady said seriously. He scarcely knew whether to be glad or sorry when he noticed tears well up in the sick man's eyes. He had never seen Mal show any emotion before. Grady felt that there was something to hope for in a man who was not too proud or self-sufficient to shed a tear. Not wishing to cause Mal embarrassment and hardly able to trust his own voice, Grady grasped Mal's shoulder in a hard grip and turned from the room.

Grady went directly to the doctor's office and

announced that he wanted to take Mal out of the hospital.

"Well," the doctor hesitated, "last week I would have said he was ready to go, but during the weekend while you were gone, he lapsed again into a depressed mood. I'm not sure he should be released yet."

"I have a theory, Doctor," Grady said, "if you will permit me —"

"Certainly, what is it, Brother Rogers?"

"I have a feeling that if I can take Mal home and stay with him myself to give him care that somehow I can find a way to break through the shell he has built around himself. If I can once get through to him with God's help I think I can get him back on the right track."

"You may be right," the doctor said. "After all, my job is to mend physical ailments, while you preachers are skilled in healing sick souls. Let's watch Smith a few days and if your idea still seems like a good one at the end of the week we'll let you take him home."

Neither man said anything to Mal about leaving the hospital. Both were quite surprised therefore when he asked the doctor one morning when he could go home. It was the first time Mal had shown any interest in getting well.

"You have been here three weeks now," the doctor said. "In another week you can start using your arm a little. Also in another week or so we can take the weights off your leg. Perhaps, if you continue to improve, by this time next week you can be released."

Mal thanked him almost cheerfully. Then the doctor asked him how he would manage at home reminding him that he would have to depend upon someone to care for him at least until he could walk again.

Grady started to offer his assistance when Mal turned toward him and said, "I thought I'd see if I could hire Brother Rogers to stay with me for a few weeks."

Nothing he could have said would have pleased Grady Rogers more. It was what he had expected to do for Mal, but he knew it was much better for Mal's morale to have made the suggestion himself. He knew also that it was not easy for Mal to be dependent upon any human being.

"I'm sure I could arrange to stay with you a while," the preacher agreed casually. "Not having any family of my own it wouldn't be any inconvenience at all for me to live with you as long as you need me."

After the doctor and Grady had left his room Mal reflected that it had never occurred to him to ask Grady about his family or how he happened to be alone. He recalled that Rosie and Hiram Jackson had occasionally mentioned that Grady had once had a child, who had died many years before. But he had never asked for any particulars.

As a matter of fact, Grady Rogers always seemed to be so taken up with the griefs and misfortunes of other people that no one gave much thought to his own problems. To Mal as he lay in his bed thinking about Grady, the man appeared to be ageless, tireless and selfless.

"I admire him. I admire him very much," he muttered aloud as a nurse came into his room. Then he surprised her further by launching into a lengthy account of the many deeds of mercy and kindness Grady had to his credit.

"You should feel very proud and secure to have such a pastor," the nurse answered.

Mal looked thoughtful and said in a far-away voice, "A pastor! Yes, a man should feel secure with a pastor like that. The whole world would be secure if it were peopled with men like that."

Whenever Grady visited Mal during the next week, he found him quite cheerful and eager to be released. On his last day in the hospital he gave Grady checks with which to pay all his bills. As soon as the hour for leaving arrived he was ready and waiting for the ambulance. In less than two hours he was lifted into his bed at home, grateful indeed to be there.

chapter 23

MAL'S MENTAL HEALTH improved at once after his return to his own home. Grady Rogers gave him the best of physical care and prayed constantly that he might help Mal to adopt a more wholesome spiritual attitude.

He went to the veteran's organization at Hartstown explaining about Mal's accident and need for a wheelchair when he was able to leave his bed sometime within the next few weeks. Not only was he able to rent the desired wheelchair, but he also secured a hospital bed with which to make the patient more comfortable while he must stay in bed.

Mal was delighted when Grady brought in the bed. The preacher set it up in the living room so that Mal could enjoy the brightness of the room as well as the cheerfulness of the fireplace. Mal would be much happier in the large, comfortable room. Grady went for Hiram Jackson to come and help him move his patient.

It was only a week before Christmas now and rough winter weather had set in. Grady moved his clothes and the books he would need for study and settled himself to live in Mal's home perhaps for the rest of the winter.

He kept up with all his regular appointments and managed to discharge his usual duties. Since Mal's house was warmed with wood fires, the sick man could not be left alone for long. Someone had to keep the fires going. However, many neighbors dropped in on Mal as he lay in bed. He was never allowed to suffer from lack of care.

One day while Mal and Grady visited before the crackling fire, Mal told Grady that he could not understand why the same ones who a few weeks before apparently were hostile toward him now were generous and gracious.

"But now you are helpless, Mal, and need the help others can give you. You would do as much for a neighbor in need whether you liked him or not, wouldn't you?" Grady framed his question deliberately, because he wanted to stir within Mal a sense of man's responsibility to others. He felt rewarded when Mal responded honestly, "I'm not sure I would, Grady. I'm afraid I have grown pretty selfish. I don't seem to care much what happens to anyone."

"While you were in the hospital there were times when you didn't seem to care what happened to yourself either," Grady pointed out gravely.

"But I did care!" Mal cried. "I wanted to die and felt impatient with anyone who tried to save my life."

Grady turned in his comfortable chair where he sat before the fireplace. He faced his companion who was raised to a half-sitting position in bed.

"Mal," Grady said gently, "something tragic has happened in your life to cause you to feel that you don't want to live. You know whether you want to talk about it or not, but as a man who has counselled individuals for more than twenty years I believe I have had experience enough that I am qualified to advise you. Talking with the right person about one's troubles helps."

"I have accepted many favors from you, Grady," Mal said shortly, "because there seems no other way, but I don't see any reason why I should burden you unnecessarily with my troubles."

For the next three days Mal was unusually quiet, thanking Grady politely for every act of kindness but responding with as few words as possible to his benefactor's attempts at conversation.

Grady himself was not as cheerful as usual. Christmas day had come and gone. It was Grady's usual custom to spend the day with the Jacksons or the Hillcrofts, but this year he had declined all invitations to stay with Mal in his helplessness. Of course, the two men imprisoned by Mal's unfortunate accident had not been forgotten nor neglected by the community.

At the annual Christmas party held in the schoolhouse, Grady had received several gifts from his friends. And on Christmas day the neighbors living close by had brought in fresh pork, cakes, pies, preserves and holiday candy.

Mal was deeply appreciative of this thoughtfulness. He had forgotten that neighbors could be so kind.

Now, however, Mal had grown morose again and Grady felt that he was to blame. Nothing he could think of to talk about seemed to arouse Mal's interest in the least. It was hard, too, for Grady, a man who loved the out-of-doors, to be cheerful constantly confined to a cabin. He enjoyed visiting with his many friends and found it difficult to maintain his usual serene outlook.

One bright day in early January he made Mal comfortable, built up the fires and announced he would be gone for awhile.

He walked slowly through the woods to Dave Gurney's store to pick up some needed groceries and enjoyed a half-hour's visit with the aging merchant. There was an unusual pallor in Dave's face and for the first time Grady saw unsteadiness in the elderly man's step. It came as a shock to see Dave faltering. He had always appeared so hearty and strong and active that one just never thought of him as growing old.

Grady left the store and went on to Rosie's house. His heart was heavy but the crisp clean air filling his lungs had an exhilarating effect. Rosie's children were in school, Hiram was at work in the woods, and she sat alone by the fire sewing for her girls.

"I'm glad you've come, Brother Rogers," she greeted. "Since you are staying with Mr. Smith we seldom see you. All of us miss your visits."

"I miss you too, Rosie. Your family seems more like my own than anyone I know."

"Well, we sure owe a plenty to you," Rosie said tenderly. Her heart was always touched by the loneliness in Grady's life. *I can't understand why such a good man who deserved the best a woman could give him should be so alone in the world,* she often thought. *But I guess he is the kind that never could love but just one woman.*

Grady, who had thought Rosie the loveliest of young girls when he first met her, often reflected that womanhood had crowned her with a gentleness and sweet serenity he had never seen in any other woman. She was a wise mother, a faithful wife and a tireless servant of the Lord.

"You look tired, Brother Rogers," she said now as she laid aside her sewing and rose to set a cup of coffee before her guest.

"I am tired, Rosie. And troubled too. I have just come from Dave's store and he seems to be ill. Have you see him lately?"

Rosie replied that she and Hiram had been much concerned about "Uncle Dave." They had urged him to come and live with them but he had stubbornly refused.

"I was shocked, too, when I saw him last week. I hadn't realized how much older he was getting. I guess I have been spending so much time worrying about Frankie—"

"And, of course, you've had no word?" Grady knew he would be the first person Rosie

would turn to outside her own family when word
came about her wounded son.

"No word at all, Brother Rogers. Sometimes
I think I can't stand it anymore. Part of the time
I feel sure he will come home again and other
times I'm sure I told him goodbye forever when he
went away." Unrestrained tears rolled down Rosie's
cheeks and Grady grieved with her. Although he
knew it was good for this worried mother to resort
once in a while to tears, like most men Grady
felt helpless to comfort a sobbing woman. To
relieve the situation he asked for another cup of
coffee.

"Surely, Brother Rogers," Rosie said cordially,
wiping her eyes and hurrying into the kitchen.
"And here is some mince pie that just finished
baking in the oven." She set the food before him
and asked how Mr. Smith was feeling. As he ate
Grady related the story of Mal's moodiness.

"He has had trouble, Rosie, but I don't
know of any way a person can help him unless he
makes up his mind to let them," Grady said.

"He will someday," Rosie assured him, "if
you will be patient to give him time. Have you ever
noticed the hurt look in his eyes?"

"You can't help it." Grady had seen the ap-
pealing and haunted look many times in Mal's fine
gray eyes. "That's the reason I can never give up
trying to help him. Only a man who has suffered much would ever look so hurt. But I must go
now. Thanks for the coffee. Hold fast to your

faith, Rosie, and some day your boy will come home to you."

"Yes, Brother Rogers, somehow I feel you are right."

"And keep a sharp eye on your Uncle Dave. I'm worried about him."

Grady walked with a spring in his step as he returned to Mal's cabin. It always did him good to visit with Rosie. He and Mal had only the usual commonplace things to say to each other as he busied himself with stirring up the fire and attending to other household chores. Mal could not help but notice the cheery note in his attitude, a note that had been missing for several days.

"Did you have a good visit with your friends this afternoon?" he inquired as they ate the supper Grady had prepared.

"Oh, yes, indeed," Grady was glad to see Mal take an interest in someone else. He rarely asked questions about any community happenings. Grady recounted his visits with Dave Gurney and Rosie Jackson. Then he continued to talk of Rosie's virtues. Before he finished he had told Mal the story of the thwarted courtship of Rosie and Hiram and how Hiram had been forced to hide out for four years until the mystery of who had killed a government agent had been solved.

"That's quite a story," Mal responded. "Sounds like something that one reads in a novel."

"I suspect that most of the stories written

as novels have really happened to folks," Grady said.

"Novels have happy endings," Mal interposed, "but too many of the stories in real life have the wrong kind of ending."

"Rosie's didn't," Grady reminded him.

"And apparently yours hasn't," Mal said.

Grady was quiet for a brief moment before replying. "Happiness is where one finds it or rather where one makes it," he said at last. "My life has been filled with many heartaches and disappointments but God has a way of making up for such things and oftentimes turns evil into good."

"You go along then with the school of thought that all things work together for good?" Mal questioned.

"The Apostle Paul once said that 'We know all things work together for good to them that love God and are the called according to His purpose.' I believe that! I've seen many adversities in my own life turned to my benefit," Grady said.

"At one time I could believe in such doctrine," Mal said bitterly. "But that was before certain things had happened to me. Now I don't know if I'll ever believe in anything again."

"Mal, my friend," Grady spoke persuasively, "that is the most mistaken idea you could possibly have. When you once believed in God and His promises you knew that you also believed that 'Neither death or life, nor angels, nor principalities, nor powers nor things present, nor things to come, nor height nor depth nor any other creature shall be able to separate us from the love of God,'" quoted Grady with a triumphant ring in his voice.

"I hadn't thought of it in that light," Mal admitted humbly. Being a man accustomed to making quick decisions, he added, "Perhaps I'd better revise my line of thinking. I've been blaming the Lord for deserting me. Maybe it's that I've deserted Him."

Grady's heart gave a glad lurch. He knew that Mal at last was back on the right track. With his usual perception, however, he realized also that there was nothing more for him to say at the moment. Just as a physician knows that the patient must reach a place where he is willing to depend upon his own resources so does the one skilled in the field of treating spiritual illness know that he can go only so far in helping the one leaning on him. Leaving Mal with his own meditations, Grady headed out toward the barn and the evening chores.

chapter 24

Neighbors visited almost daily in the Smith cabin during Mal's long days of convalescence. Among them were Mandy and John Hillcroft, John Gurney, Hiram and Rosie Jackson and their family, and the Goodman girls.

Mal was quite sure that they came more to see Grady Rogers than because of their interest in him. And he could not blame them. Certainly he had known no person in his life who had such a real interest in other people as Grady Rogers.

Of all the persons who came Mal liked the visits of Mary Goodman and Rosie Jackson the best. That is, next to the visits paid him by Ann Goodman.

Mal considered Ann's visits apart from all the others. Her visits almost invariably coincided with the periods when Grady Rogers was absent. This suited Mal because he was sure Ann's visits would not be as pleasant if shared with someone else. This arrangement was also satisfactory to Grady. He thoroughly disapproved of Ann Goodman and had never attempted to conceal the fact.

Ann was one person in the valley who disliked Grady Rogers intensely. It was not because he disapproved of her, however, for Ann never cared at all for any person's approval or disapproval.

But she did care about being made to feel a person less worthwhile than her capabilities afforded. An encounter with Grady Rogers always made her feel that way in spite of her best efforts to shrug off her sense of guilt.

Even though Ann's presence gave Mal pleasure, she invariably left him feeling restless and uncertain. He never mentioned her comings and goings to Grady. Mal did not know what his friend and benefactor thought of the girl because they had never discussed her.

During these days Grady found his patient to be growing much more companionable. If he did not talk of Ann, he did have much to say of her sister Mary and Rosie Jackson.

The two of them often came together to pick up clothes to be laundered, and to do bits of housecleaning here and there. Or if there was nothing to be done they sat by the fire in the large cheery room. Brilliant shafts of sunlight gleamed through the spacious undressed windows, for Mal had fought tenaciously against all the efforts of well-meaning neighborhood women to put curtains to the windows. He wanted only the properly fit draperies to keep the room from looking bare. There must be nothing to shut out the light, sunshine and the wonderful, ever-changing, ever-interesting, ever-satisfying view.

He had discussed the subject briefly with Hiram once when he had first moved into the house.

"Yes," Hiram agreed. "That's something hard to understand about womenfolk. When you are building a house they howl their heads off for lots of windows and then they turn around and shut out all the light and sunshine with curtains and stuff."

Mal never knew when he began noticing Mary Goodman. She was one of the first persons to come to see him after he returned from the hospital. However, she never came alone, but always in the company of Rosie or Mandy Hill-croft. She invariably brought some delicious bit of food with her and could always find something to do about the house that would contribute to the comfort of the two bachelors who dwelt there.

Her entrance into the house was quiet and unobtrusive, her conversation easy. Always she moved about the rooms with grace and dignity. One could scarcely enumerate her activities while in the house nor could one recall anything she had said, yet when she was gone the room seemed strangely empty and Mal felt a sense of loneliness.

Of course, Mal did not spend much time thinking about these things. He did not permit himself to think much about any person principally because there was no one who aroused his interest — except Ann Goodman, and she simply amused him in a vague sort of way. Mal found himself wondering many times a day when Ann would come to see him. Whenever he heard footsteps approaching or a rap on the door, he hoped it would

be Ann. Somehow, he was disappointed and irritated when it turned out to be someone else.

He had progressed now to the wheelchair.
It had been necessary for him to be returned to
the hospital for the removal of the cast on his
leg. Grady, of course, had accompanied him in
the ambulance and both men were glad for the
diversion the trip afforded them.

The winter weather had been rough and
temperatures had been low compared to the usual
Ozark weather. Now, everyone, a little bored with
the uneventful weeks was eagerly looking forward
to spring. Seed catalogs were arriving in the mail
and suggestions for early planting and seed bed
preparations were being broadcast daily on farm
radio programs.

Mal would soon be able to care for himself
and Grady looked forward to going home. He had
sacrificed many personal interests to attend to Mal's
needs and comforts, but on the other hand the
generous wages Mal had given him had solved some
knotty financial problems for him.

He and Mal had done a great deal of good
reading throughout the long weeks of forced in-
activity. They had many pleasant discussions, but
Grady had not been able, so far as he knew, to lead
Mal back to God and restore his faith.

Mal had made encouraging progress, however. His spells of melancholy moodiness were almost a thing of the past and his conversational remarks were much less bitter. Still, he had never

opened up and told Grady the things that happened to him to cause him to bury himself in this isolated country. Then one day it happened, just a week before Grady was to go home. He had gone to the post office and to see his friend, Dave Gurney and had learned two pieces of news on the trip, both from Dave.

"I'm giving up the post office and store, Grady," the old man announced. "Just can't seem to hold out no longer."

"I'm sorry, Dave, but of course, you know best. Who will take over for you?"

"Yes, Grady, I guess old Dave ain't long for this world. I been a failin' now for quite a spell. Rosie's been a tryin' to get me to sell out everything and go live with her and Hiram, but I ain't a goin' to do that," the old man said determinedly.

"And I told Rosie I wasn't going to sell my stuff neither. I ain't got nobody but Rosie and John. He ain't got many years left either so he don't need nothin'. So I'm just goin' to turn everything over to Rosie and Hiram. Sure wish Frankie were home because I always expected him to help me out."

Grady felt miserable as he watched the feebleness of this burly old man before him. "I'm sorry, Dave," he repeated. "If there is anything I can do to help—"

"There's nothin', Grady. I ain't afraid to go wherever the good Lord wants me. I'll just go on and wait on the other side for you and all my other friends who'll be comin' along one of these days."

At the conclusion of this remark, Dave brightened. "I'd sure be proud if you could come over next Monday and help Rosie and Hiram take inventory. They'll have to know how much stuff they have here to keep their records straight for the government."

"Yes, I know!" Grady replied. "And I'll be glad to help."

"I mind the time when a man could run his business to suit himself without the government getting nosey about everything," Dave remarked grumpily and Grady smiled indulgently.

Another thing Dave had to talk about was a registered letter addressed to a John Smith.

"Looks like a woman's writing," Dave expounded perusing the address on it, "but I don't know no John Smith. I reckon I'll have to return it."

Grady looked at the letter and noticed that the postmark was a county seat in the northern part of the state. He handed the letter back to Dave.

"Smith is a common name, Dave," he advised. "I'd keep the letter a day or so. Maybe someone will call for it."

As he strolled leisurely home from the post office, Grady recalled that Mal Smith had once in his delirium in the hospital insisted that his name was not Mal but John. He determined to tell Mal about the letter.

When Grady reached home, Mal Smith already had a guest. It was Mary Goodman, who had come from Rosie Jackson to tell Grady that at long last a message had come from Frankie. He was being flown back to the United States to a hospital in California. He had a leg injury, but he was out of danger. He would be home on a furlough sometime within a month.

Rosie, herself, had been sick in bed for two days with influenza. When the telegram came she had sent Mary, who was nursing her, to bring the good news.

Mary knocked at the kitchen door and entered timidly when she heard a voice say, "Come in."

"Oh," she said to Mal when she saw he was alone. "I thought Brother Rogers would be here. I've come to tell him Hiram and Rosie have heard from Frankie. Rosie was sick and couldn't come."

Mal thought Mary made a pretty picture standing before him, her soft brown eyes aglow with the excitement of the good news. Her cheeks were rosy red from exercise. She unmistakably was disappointed and baffled not to find Grady at home. For some unaccountable reason Mal, in a more facetious mood than he had felt for many months, felt impelled to tease.

"No, he has gone to the post office," Mal drawled smiling. "But won't I do just as well?"

Mary caught the gleam of amusement in his

eye and thought, *Mr. Smith must be getting a lot better. I've never see him smile before.*

"Well," she faltered, "Rosie is sick in bed but she wanted Brother Rogers to know right away, so I came over to tell him."

"Oh, yes, indeed," Mal responded with mock seriousness. He had not the slightest notion what Mary was trying to say. "Won't you sit down, please, and tell me all about it?" The tantalizing look still shone in his eyes and Mary thought, *Strange I never noticed how handsome he is before this.*

She sank into a deep chair near the fires and pushed back her coat. "Hiram went to Hartstown this morning and someone over there—I don't know who—gave him this telegram. He drove back as fast as he could to tell Rosie and now she's laughing and crying all over the place. I came to tell Brother Rogers," she repeated.

"And do you always get so confused when you deliver a message that you forget to tell what the message is?"

"Oh, my goodness," Mary squealed, "Frankie is safe. He is coming home."

"And that good news made his mother ill?"

"No, no, no," Mary laughed heartily. "She was already sick. I've been staying with her for two days."

Then she turned on Mal slightly furious. "I wouldn't make such a mess of—of—telling things if you didn't look at me like that."

"Like what?" Mal was merciless.

"Like you were teasing. Like you were making fun of me."

"Oh, I'm sorry, Mary. Really. I never saw you so pretty — so — so alive," Mal said seriously. "I couldn't help teasing but I didn't mean to offend you. I hope you will forgive me."

"But I've never seen you like this either. You have always seemed so — so —" Mary hesitated afraid to go on.

"So what, Mary?" Mal urged.

"Pigheaded!" Mary said impulsively and then gasped. "Oh, I'm sorry. I didn't mean that. I don't know what's the matter with me."

She rose and started to button her coat. "I must go —"

But Mal urged her to stay. "Please don't go," he begged. "Why do you call me pigheaded?"

"Oh, I didn't mean that at all. I'm so sorry I said it," Mary was terribly embarrassed. She wanted nothing so much as to get away but something in Mal's pleading made her sit down again.

"Tell me just exactly what you did mean. You sort of owe me an explanation, don't you think?" he wheedled.

"Yes. Yes, I do. It's just that you have come here to forget something that has hurt you and — well, instead of forgetting you've just kept your grief inside you — nursed it along. You've rejected every effort of good and kind people who would have helped you."

"Rejected whose efforts?" Mal asked quietly.

"Rosie Jackson and Grady Rogers and — and — me. I could have helped you, but you thought you could do everything by yourself."

Mal supposed he should be angry, but he wasn't. In the first place he knew Mary was telling the truth and he strongly suspected that she did not ordinarily confront others so frankly with their shortcomings.

"You are being a little unfair when you say I have rejected Grady Roger's attempts to help me. I shall never be able to repay him," Mal was serious now. "He has cared for me as a father would a son."

"But you did reject his advice until sickness and misfortune forced you to accept his help," Mary was defensively stubborn.

"Various circumstances in life force us into many of our attitudes and tendencies, don't they?" Mal wanted to know.

"Yes, that's true," Mary agreed thoughtfully recalling unhappy instances in her own life.

"And I have never rejected Grady Roger's advice," Mal went on to say, "because he doesn't give advice. He only points the way and leaves the person to decide which way he will go. And all the while he lives as selflessly as I have ever seen any human being live. I have never seen anyone like him."

"Neither has anyone else," Mary said. "I

wish there could be more people in the world like him."

"The many weeks that I have lived with him have taught me much about myself. He has caused me to take such an interest in other people that I have been able to forget a large part of my own hurt. But better than that he has shown me the way back to God."

Just then Grady Rogers came into the room. He greeted Mary and stepped across the room to stir up the fire.

"We were just talking about you," Mal said.

"And what were you saying? Something good, I hope."

"Very good," Mary said quickly. "Mr. Smith just got through saying he was going to start going to church."

"Did you say that, Mal?"

"No, I didn't," Mal replied looking accusingly at Mary. The deep flush in her countenance amused him while Grady wondered about the twinkle in his eyes.

"But I *am* going to go back to church," he continued facing Grady and speaking soberly.

"I'm glad, Mal. Oh, so very glad."

"I wish you'd sit down, Grady," Mal said. "I have a story I'd like to tell you and Mary."

Mal began with his marriage to Kathy and his struggle to become established in a successful law practice. Then he told about his call into the air force and his subsequent experiences there, ending with his dramatic return to find Kathy married and lost to him forever. He told the story simply without sentiment and without emotion. His part in the telling was as detached as though he were talking of somone he had known in another world.

Grady Rogers was visibly moved by the tragic tale while tears coursed unchecked down Mary's face.

"Oh, to think of all the cruel unjust things people have said," she cried. "Nobody ever dreamed you had suffered so much. Can you ever forgive us?"

"I can understand and understanding helps one to forgive, I guess. And besides, I have made little effort to be friendly," Mal replied.

"I am very sorry for all that has happened to you," Grady said, directing his words to Mal. "I too must apologize for some of the things I have had to say. Which goes to remind us that we should not be hasty to judge another."

After Mary went soberly down the trail to her home Mal and Grady sat talking while the sun set and evening shadows dropped a soft black mantle about the hills around them. Grady told Mal of the letter Dave had for a John Smith and mentioned the cancelled post mark.

"That's my former home," Mal replied. "So I'm quite sure the letter is for me."

chapter 25

THE LETTER FOR MAL, which was the first
one that he had received in the many months he
had been living in Clear Springs, was from Judge
Dalton. The old man had wheedled Mal's address
from Mal's attorney. The following message greeted
Mal when he opened the envelope:

Dear John,

A letter from me will be surprising to you
no doubt and I apologize for trespassing upon your
desire for privacy. However, I seem to have no
choice, but to do what I must and I pray your
forgiveness.

The situation is simply this: Kathy is quite
ill in a private sanitarium. She knows she will never
get well and her only concern is for the welfare
of her child and that before she dies she can know
that you have forgiven her.

I know that it is asking an awful lot and I
shall not attempt to persuade you. But because of
her constant pleadings I promised I would write to
you.

Kathy seems to have no doubts that you will
adopt her daughter as your own child because you
are a Christian. She asks you in the same spirit
to forgive the great suffering she brought upon you.

Neil Hamilton deserted Kathy when the
child was born and later permitted her to obtain a
divorce giving her custody of the child. Since then
Hamilton has taken his own life with an overdose of
sleeping pills.

Kathy has no one to whom to turn in her
illness and helplessness. I am an old man broken

in spirit and financially as well. One of my boys had to have help getting started when he returned from the war. He was discharged due to an emotional instability. He has been a great expense and constant source of worry to me. The other two are still in the service, but Gerald's wife has had some serious operations that have cost me nearly a fortune. So you see I am in poor circumstances to offer Kathy advice or assistance. Her baby girl is being cared for by a private family whom I am paying.

Kathy feels that you might be inclined to assume responsibility for the child, although I must confess I see no reason why you should do so and have repeatedly said as much to Kathy. However, she has remained obdurate and talks of nothing else, explaining that I just don't know the Christian spirit that dwells in you.

Although her physicians hold out little hope for her recovery they thought it much better for her if her mind is put at ease. They urged me to contact you in her behalf.

Can you, will you, come to see Kathy and explain to her yourself how you feel about this matter?

Respectfully,
G. S. Dalton

Grady had disappeared toward the barn to do the evening chores after delivering Mal's letter.

While reading the letter Mal's face turned livid white, a coloring which changed to a choleric purple as he read on. Grady thought he looked quite apopleptic when he came into the room. In fact, Mal was so visibly disturbed that Grady decided not to inquire about the letter.

He replenished the fire to warm the cooling room and retired to the kitchen to prepare a warm supper. Mal, however, refused to eat. Thereupon Grady tidied up the kitchen and excused himself choosing to spend the evening with the Hillcrofts rather than to sit with Mal as long as he was in such a dark mood. Perhaps when he had had a few hours to get hold of himself he would be better company.

Grady had thought he would have the pleasure of telling Mandy and John Hillcroft of Frankie Jackson's safety and that the boy would soon be home, but Mary Goodman had stopped there on her way from Mal's and told them the good news. Although Mal had not asked Mary and Grady to keep the things he had told them in confidence, the good breeding of each of them kept them from indulging in idle gossip concerning his past.

When Grady returned to the cabin Mal was in a much better frame of mind. He apologized to Grady for his surliness and handed him the letter, asking him to read it.

When Grady finished reading he returned it to Mal and said, "You'll need time to think about a request of that sort before replying."

"What do you mean?" Mal replied savagely. "Haven't I had enough without having to play the role of father to Neil Hamilton's child?"

"Yes, I'd say you have been through quite enough," Grady said quietly, "but in the end you'll have to do what your conscience tells you to do."

"Why should I have a conscience toward Neil Hamilton?"

Grady was glad to hear Mal talk. It was so much better for the man than sullen silence and brooding. He was quite sure that Mal Smith must have been a devout and consecrated Christian at one time in his life. Otherwise his wife would not have been so confident of his acceptance of her child. Grady could easily sense the struggle that was going on within the man.

Grady persuaded Mal to talk at great length about Kathy that night before they finally went to bed. From the conversation he deducted that Mal had actually "gotten over" Kathy and had forgiven her part in the unfortunate affair. Still, his heart was full of hatred for Neil Hamilton.

After assisting Mal to his bed and giving him a sedative to make him rest, Grady went to his bed with a new problem to solve — that of trying to help Mal Smith find himself. *If I can only help him re-establish his faith in God he will have the means of fighting against the evils that beset him,* thought Grady.

chapter 26

GRADY reached Dave Gurney's store early the following Monday morning but Dave, Rosie and Hiram were already there ahead of him, busy with pad and pencil listing the items of stock in the country store.

The foursome spent the entire day at their task, taking a few minutes out for a noon lunch.

Rosie watched her uncle anxiously and had many misgivings in her heart regarding his apparent cheerfulness and well being. When Dave insisted upon going with Hiram and his niece next day to Hartstown to get the legal details of transferring his property disposed of, she tried to persuade him to wait until he had rested a few days.

"Plenty of time for rest later, Rosie," he said. "I want this business all taken care of as soon as we can get it done while there is still time."

"But I thought you wanted Frankie to have the store," Hiram interrupted. "He'll be home soon now. Why not wait until then if you still want to make it legal as you call it?"

"There's no time for waiting," Dave insisted. "I know what I'm doing. I did hope once upon a time that I could turn this business over to Frankie but the more I think and pray about it the more I am beginning to believe that Frankie is coming home to preach. Some of these days Brother Rogers is going to have to have somebody to take his place and I figure Frankie will do it all right, if he can spend a few years studying and practicing with Brother Rogers."

Dave spoke quietly and with assurance. It was as though he had a premonition of things to come. The three persons to whom he was speaking listened quietly and let him have his way.

So the following day the whole party went in Hiram's truck to Hartstown and all of Dave's property was transferred to Rosie and Hiram and their heirs with one stipulation. Dave was to maintain possession of his home until the hour of his death.

Grady was invited to go along and took advantage of the opportunity to buy some needed supplies for himself and Mal. When the group returned to Clear Springs Dave appeared to be very tired. However, he insisted on relieving his brother John who had taken care of the store during their absence.

He dismissed Hiram and Rosie to go home and do their chores, admonishing them that they would have to get up early to be on hand to open the store next morning.

"Oh," Rosie said, "I thought you would open up mornings." Then she stopped to think. "But, of course, if you don't feel like it, Uncle Dave," she spoke softly.

"I feel just as good as anyone else," her

uncle barked, "but this store belongs to you and Hiram and I ain't going to be snooping around telling you how to run it."

Tears filled Rosie's eyes and she kissed Dave on the forehead. "We'll need you to tell us how to run it," she said seriously. "We sure don't know much about buying and selling goods."

"You'll learn," Dave replied. "Now run along, child. Everything will be all right."

Rosie smiled through her tears and told her uncle "goodbye." She left the store reluctantly, for Dave's manner disturbed her.

"I never thought I'd live to see him give up," she said to Grady Rogers as they bumped along in the truck over the rough road home.

"He don't act like a man that's give up exactly," Hiram said, "but more like he has finished his job and is ready for something new to happen."

"Don't worry about him, Rosie," Grady advised. "I used to go over often to spend evenings with him, but since I've been staying in with Mal, I haven't had an opportunity to do so. Now that Mal can look after himself better I can get away so I'll just run over and see him after supper."

Rosie felt relieved and said so. She and Hiram invited Grady to have supper with them but he excused himself because he needed to get home and do the evening chores as well as prepare supper for Mal.

He was relieved to find his companion

in a conversational mood. Mal had retreated once more into a sullen silence since the day Grady had delivered Kathy's letter.

"You seem to be feeling much better," he remarked as they sat eating supper.

Mal was getting about the house quite well on his crutches now and could even get himself into bed without assistance.

"I made a discovery today that changes many things for me," Mal replied seriously. "I find that I have gotten over Kathy quite completely. But I shall always hate Neil Hamilton."

"I'm sorry that you have not found that you have 'gotten over' Hamilton too," Grady said. "Hatred is a cankerous thing that eats at the heart and soul of a man."

Grady and Mal talked of other things, because as counsellor and confidant, the minister knew how easily one could say too much or inquire too curiously into personal affairs. Better to let Mal volunteer any confidences rather than to prod him with questions.

Grady excused himself early and left to go to see Dave, without stopping to clear the table and put the kitchen in order. Dave welcomed him gladly. "Was just sittin' here wishin' you'd come like you used to, Brother Rogers," he said. "I feel the need for someone to talk to tonight."

The conversation for the whole evening was about Rosie and Hiram and the future of their children, especially Frankie.

However, before the evening was over they fell to talking of funerals and coffin-making. Grady was never able afterward to recall which one of them brought up the subject but Dave recounted instance after instance when he had made the coffin for a deceased friend or relative.

"I reckon I've made over a hundred coffins in my time," he said simply. "And now you come with me and I'll show you the one I've got fixed up for myself."

Dave rose from his chair and led Grady into a short hall. At the end was a door. Here he took keys from his pocket and unlocked a padlock. The room they entered was a bedroom musty-smelling and stale, but furnished with beautiful old-fashioned cherry furniture. There resting on wooden saw-horses was a huge unpolished walnut casket.

"It's beautiful, Dave," was all Grady could say.

"Ain't nobody ever seen it but you and my brother John," Dave said, rubbing his hand tenderly over the mellowed wood so expertly put together. "Lots of folks is superstitious about death and coffins and such. Rosie'd have a fit if she knew what was in this room."

Grady was anxious to get away from what seemed to him a gloomy room, but Dave wanted to linger.

"Ma and Pa both died here in this room," he said reverently. "Pa first and then Ma. It's just like it was when she left it. Now when I go they'll lay me out in here."

Rarely at a loss for words, Grady could think of no appropriate remark to make. He merely nodded his head sympathetically and eased his host out of the room.

At ten o'clock Grady bade Dave Gurney "good night," not knowing that he was to be the last person to speak to him on this earth.

The next morning when Hiram and Rosie came to open the store they stopped first to see him and found him dead in his bed.

chapter 27

THE COMMUNITY was shocked beyond belief at the news of Dave's death.

"He tried every way he could to tell us he was goin'," Rosie mourned, "and no one paid him any heed. How dreadful that he had to be all alone."

"Oh, I don't know Rosie, girl," her father comforted. "I reckon it's a heap better to have death slip up on you easy like than to have to sit around and wait for it."

"I guess Dave was the best friend I ever had," Hiram declared shaking his head. "I reckon I never did think about him a dyin' even when he was talking so much about it yesterday."

As so often happens, trouble did not come singly. Scarcely had they come to accept Dave's death when the people of the valley received further unhappiness. On the day of Dave's funeral Mrs. Goodman was stricken seriously ill. Two days after that Mary received word that her husband's father was starting proceedings to take her child, Jody, from her.

Mary, frightened, grieved and benumbed with the shock of such a turn of events, turned to Grady Rogers for comfort and advice. Grady felt almost as helpless as Mary herself, but naturally, was able to reason more clearly.

"This looks very bad, Mary," he said. "Tell me about your husband's father. What is he like that he would do a thing like this?"

"I don't know him," Mary replied. "I married his son, Leroy, while we were both in service. It was one of those impulsive things that happen so often in time of war. I was lonely and Leroy was nice. We had good times together and then he got his orders to go overseas. I suppose we thought we were in love and Leroy said that more than anything else he wanted a child. We decided to get married so that we could have as much time together as possible before he left me.

"Leroy was killed on D-Day in Normandy. He never knew about—" Mary hesitated, then quickly finished in a tone so low it was scarcely more than a whisper, "He never knew about Jody."

"I've told you all this before, Brother Rogers," she explained, "and there's nothing more I can tell now. Leroy never talked about his father. He told me his mother died when he was born and his father never remarried. He was the only child."

"You were discharged from the army when you were married, of course," Grady suggested.

"Yes. I was living in Kansas City with Ann who also was discharged from the army for—" again Mary seemed hesitant as though scarcely knowing how to proceed, "for physical reasons," she finished, flushing.

"I see," Grady said kindly. "And I'll do all I can to help you, Mary, but I must admit I scarcely know where to begin. I'll talk with Mal. Perhaps he can help. If he can be persuaded, would you like for him to take your case?"

"Brother Rogers, I'm so worried and scared I can't think. I know everyone in this community asks too much from you but if I could just depend on you it would help so much."

"You can depend on me, Mary. I'll do everything possible I can think to do to help," Grady repeated. "In the meantime you try to rest . Everything will work out for the best. Remember God's ways are the best ways. Put your trust in Him."

"I do, Brother Rogers, I do. And I'm grateful to you for being such a good friend."

While Mary was talking to Grady Rogers, Mal had gone to the Goodman home to inquire about Mrs. Goodman's condition and to see if he could be of any help.

He found Ann sitting on the front porch alone while her mother slept under the influence of a sedative.

"I'm sorry about your mother, Ann. Is there some way I can help?" Mal asked simply seating himself in the porch swing beside Ann.

"Mamma is better today. Only quiet and absolute rest will help her. The doctor says she has angina pectoris. It's awfully painful, I guess. We do not allow her to even turn herself in bed without assistance. No one can see her except Mary and I and Rosie who helps to care for her."

Mal nodded his sympathy.

"But we have a trouble now almost harder to bear than having Mamma sick," Ann continued.

"And what is that?"

"Mary has been notified that her father-in-law has started proceedings to obtain custody of her child. Mary—both of us—are nearly scared to death."

"Why, that is preposterous," Mal declared. "Who is her father-in-law and why does he think he can take her child from her?"

"His name is Morgan, of course, the same as Mary's. F. Monroe Morgan. We know nothing of him. Mary never even saw him."

"But he can't take the child from his mother. No court of justice on earth could do that," Mal protested.

"Couldn't they prove a mother to be unfit or something of that sort?" Ann asked.

"Some mothers, yes, but not Mary. She gives splendid care to Jody," Mal answered. "I don't think you have much to worry about. Mary can get a good attorney and he will see that she gets justice."

"Aren't you a good attorney?" Ann questioned.

"I was an attorney, but I'm no longer practicing," Mal replied shortly. "However, I can put

Mary in touch with someone who will win this case for her."

Mal rose to leave, but Ann asked from where she sat, "Then you won't take the case for us?"

Mal shook his head, "I'm sorry, Ann, but my days of law practicing are over. I've made that resolve and I intend to stick with it."

"In that case," Ann declared, "I have something more to tell you. Perhaps you can give me the proper advice. However, I tell you with the reservation that you will never under any circumstances betray my confidence."

"You can trust me," Mal said indifferently. He did not have much interest in Ann's story but still he was curious to find out if Ann was concealing any information. He needed help to unravel the mystery in his mind in regard to the habeas corpus action against such a person as Mary.

If Mal had only a cursory interest in Ann's story in the beginning his mind soon snapped to attentive interest. He listened without interrupting, but Ann could tell from the dark look on his countenance that he was outraged.

When she finished he still made no comment but stared darkly in front of him. Many times before he had been angry with Ann. At other times when they were together he had felt warmly attracted to her. Those had been enjoyable times and he had even begun to wonder if he might not someday fall in love with her — if he ever dared permit himself to love any woman. On his way to Ann's home that afternoon he had felt genuine concern for Ann because of her mother's illness — an urge to comfort her. Now, after hearing the terrible secret she had kept hidden for so long he saw her as the cold, calculating, weak, selfish and utterly ruthless person that she was. He knew that whatever tenderness for her had been aroused within him was destroyed by the time she had told him her story.

"Mal, Mal, why don't you say something? Don't just sit there," Ann pleaded when she had finished. Mal sat staring ahead of him.

"I have nothing to say," he replied coldly.

"But don't you understand, Mal? I wanted you to understand. I hoped you would."

"I am afraid I understand that all women are deceitful and treacherous. Only you seem to be more so than most and I want nothing to do with you," Mal said. "Now if you will excuse me, I shall be going. Good day."

"Remember you promised not to betray my confidence." Ann stood up, quite angry herself now.

"A promise I shall cheerfully disregard, if in telling it I can help Mary retain custody of Jody. She has been made to suffer enough."

"She has been made to suffer!" Ann screamed. "Why must Mary have all the sympathy? What about my suffering? Do you think it has been easy all of these months? I am the one who stands to lose all — Mother, Jody and — and you."

"Me?" Mal repeated. "What do you mean?"

"I love you, Mal. That's what I mean." Ann's words came in her low clear voice. "That's the reason I had to tell you. I have never really loved but two persons in my life — you and Mother! Mother is slipping away from me — and you are in love with someone else!"

Mixed emotions tumbled around in Mal's mind. The only tenderness he had ever seen in Ann was found in her regard and concern for her mother. He had often heard others remark that Ann loved only herself and her mother. But now he was incensed that Ann or anyone else should have the boldness to declare her love for him or to accuse him of being in love. So enraged was he, in fact, that he lost something of his usual poise and self control. Seizing Ann by her arms, he shook her roughly. "How dare you make such a statement? I am not in love with anyone but if I were it would be a personal affair and strictly none of your business. Do you understand?"

As quickly as it had come, his fury was spent. He took his hands from her, feeling a little foolish that he had permitted her to ruffle him.

"Of course it is none of my business. But just the same you are in love. You're in love with my sister Mary."

Mal turned and started down the steps. Ann stopped him by standing fast in front of him.

Laying her hand on his arm, she said earnestly, "It's true, Mal. It is in the way you look at Mary and in the way you say her name. Believe me, if I didn't know my chances were hopeless I'd never give you up. You're the only man I've ever seen that I wanted and usually what I want I take. But you are different. I know I can never have you."

"I'm sorry, Ann," Mal said meekly. "If you didn't always manage to infuriate me perhaps we could at least be friends."

"I don't want to be friends," Ann replied. "I want you to look at me as you look at Mary. And I want you to care for me as you sooner or later will realize you care for Mary. If I can't have you like that I don't want you at all. Now go please. I hope I never see you again."

With these words, Ann released her hold on Mal and walked straight and tall into the house.

chapter 28

AFTER TALKING WITH MARY and promising her that he would ask Mal to take her case, Grady lost no time in approaching Mal with his request. He discovered that Mal was resolved not to begin again to practice law. All the preacher's attempts at persuasion failed to move the man. He stood gazing out at the scenery through the big living room window.

"Ann Goodman asked me this afternoon to take the case," Mal related, "and I refused — just as I still refuse. If I took this case it wouldn't be long until others would be asking me to help them. Soon there would be no stopping place. Besides, I have information in this case that makes it impossible for me to defend Mary," Mal stated.

Grady was much taken aback by Mal's statement. He could scarcely keep from asking Mal what he knew. He had thought all the details of the case were common knowledge. He contented himself with suggesting, "Don't you feel that if you know anything about the case in question that would help Mary you should divulge it?"

"Mary knows all the circumstances but she prefers to keep the secret to protect other people, especially her mother. It would scarcely be fair to

243

ask her for information she doesn't wish to give out."

Grady nodded thoughtfully. "No, of course not. What do you think are the chances that Mary will win this fight?"

"Very good, I should say offhand. It's very hard to take a child from its natural parent. It depends, of course, a great deal on the cause of action, what the arguments are, and the judge of the court," Mal continued. "Do you know him? What is his reputation?"

"He's a political puppet, I'm sorry to say," Grady responded. "I hate to see this case brought before him. He has been on the bench for many years — pushed around so much that now in his dotage he doesn't know the meaning of justice."

Mal stared thoughtfully out the window.

"It has occurred to me that perhaps if the right person went to this man Morgan and talked to him man to man that perhaps he could be persuaded to drop this suit," Grady pointed out. "What do you think?"

"An excellent idea! And you are just the one to do it, Grady. Come back and let me know how you come out. I'll contact a good man in Springfield to do some checking and investigating. Do you know when the hearing has been set?"

"April 15. Just ten days from today," Grady replied.

"That doesn't give us much time. Where

does this man Morgan live — Kansas City or St. Louis?" Mal inquired.

"In Clayton, a suburb of St. Louis. If I can get into Springfield in the morning I can reach St. Louis by bus or train tomorrow night. I can see Mr. Morgan and be back here day after tomorrow or the next day."

When he reached St. Louis, Grady Rogers went directly to see a friend of his, a boyhood chum now pastor of a large church. Grady planned to make inquiries about Mary's father-in-law and thought if he knew a few pertinent facts he could better judge the kind of approach to make.

His minister friend was not able to furnish much information. He told Grady that he had heard of Morgan as had most people living in St. Louis. He was something of a political potentate, but he, the minister, was not even sure what his political activities were. The minister did mention, however, that a member of his congregation, a Mrs. Al Farnum, was active in the League of Women Voters and could probably help Grady. The minister called Mrs. Farnum and made an appointment for Grady to see her.

The lady in question received Grady Rogers graciously and gave him rapt attention while he related what he knew of the facts of Mary's marriage and the birth of her child. When he had finished Mrs. Farnum shook her head and said, "Mr. Rogers, you are up against someone pretty tough I'm afraid. Mr. Morgan is not a great power in himself, but he is in a vicious political ring here that has a lot of power throughout the state."

"Do you know anything about him personally, Mrs. Farnum? About his family or about the character of the man?" Grady asked.

"No, I have never met him. He comes from one of the pioneer families who built St. Louis — a family that has been up and down through the years. When his boy was killed in the war I read the account in the paper. There was nothing said of a wife or child as I recall, though. If it was there I would most likely have seen it. I make it a point to read the paper closely since I hold a responsible office in the League of Women Voters," Mrs. Farnum explained.

"I see," Grady rose to go. "I'll see what else I can find out about Mr. Morgan. Thanks very much for your kindness."

"I only hope this young mother and child will not be hurt in this case," Mrs. Farnum said as she walked to the door with Grady.

"My hope is that Mr. Morgan can be persuaded to drop the case," Grady replied. And then with a "goodbye" to his hostess he was on his way to see F. Monroe Morgan.

Grady went first to the man's downtown office and was told that Mr. Morgan had gone out for lunch and would not return to the office until 1:30 in the afternoon. When Grady went back to the office later in the afternoon he was informed that Mr. Morgan was in conference and had no time for an interview that day.

Determined to see the man, Grady went to his spacious house at 7 o'clock that night. He was received by Mr. Morgan in a library filled with books and heavy expensive furnishings. Grady got right to the point, explaining who he was and that he had come in Mary's interest, his daughter-in-law.

"Daughter-in-law?" Mr. Morgan exploded. He was a large, dark complexioned man of about sixty years of age. "She's no daughter-in-law of mine. I've never seen her."

"But she married your son, sir. She must be your daughter-in-law."

"Just a trick! Just a trick!" the man roared. "She made my son marry her. I knew nothing of his marriage."

"The war—the shortness of time—made many young couples marry in haste," Grady said. "Did your son not inform you of his marriage before he went overseas?"

"No, not a word. He'd have been ashamed to have told me of marrying a girl like this. She tricked him, I say."

"Then how did you learn of his marriage?" Grady wanted to know.

"From one of his buddies who was with him when he died. He knew all about it and when he came back here he told me. I've had an awful time finding the girl."

"And how did you find her?"

"I've had detectives working on it for more than a year. We didn't have any trouble finding her military record, but she seemed to drop from the earth after her discharge." The old man was blustery and boastful. He seemed to enjoy talking about his ability to track down the girl.

"I'm curious to know why you wanted to find her. You seem to hold such hatred for her," Grady ventured.

"Certainly I hate her. I had plans for my son. The war delayed them somewhat. I could have kept him at home, but he seemed determined to go — enlisted, in fact. As soon as he was old enough."

"I see," Grady said. "And you were anxious to find the girl for what reasons?"

"Because I suspected that she made him marry her because she was going to have a child. And if that child was alive and I could find it I was going to have him."

"Why?" Grady asked.

"Because my son Leroy was the last of the Morgans. We've been a great family — a family of builders and fighters." The old man sat staring before him for a moment as though his mind were reviewing years of exploits and adventures of the Morgan family.

Then he raised his head and looked steadily at Grady as he explained, "More than anything else in the world I have planned for Leroy to have sons to carry on his family name."

"But by what right do you claim this child? Surely the mother is—"

"Right!" Mr. Morgan roared. "Every right in the world. Isn't he my own flesh and blood? Isn't it enough that I gave my only son in the service of his country?"

"But what about the mother? You can scarcely argue that you have the greater right than she to the child," Grady interposed.

"I certainly can offer the child better advantages than an ignorant nobody from the hills," Mr. Morgan stormed. "I have wealth, I have power. I can give him everything!"

"Everything but a mother's care and devotion, Mr. Morgan. I'm afraid the court will think that is pretty important."

"A proper mother, yes, Mr. Rogers, but certainly it is hardly to be expected that a family of such influence and power as the Morgans would be expected to permit a grandson to be raised in a part of the country that is wild and scarcely civilized."

"How do you propose to prove Mary Morgan is an improper mother?" Grady insisted. "She has a fine reputation. I have known her since she was a child. You can't find a flaw in her character."

"But who will testify in her behalf?" the old man asked.

"I will," Grady responded. "And so will dozens of others."

"If you are not disqualified," Mr. Morgan returned.

"Disqualified!" Grady was incredulous. "You wouldn't dare. I have every right in the world to testify at that hearing and I intend to do so!"

"Mr. Rogers," his host said smoothly. "Have you come here to try to persuade me not to carry out this habeas corpus proceedings or to threaten me?"

"I came to try to show you how wrong you are," Grady returned firmly. "But I can see it is useless. Threatening and brow beating is not my way of doing, but I warn you fairly and squarely that if you go through with these unholy and unrighteous proceedings that you had better be prepared for fireworks. We're not going to accept this bit of injustice without putting up a fight!"

Both men were standing now facing each other. Grady strove to maintain his self-control and to keep his voice calm. He detected a faint gleam of fear in the eyes of F. Monroe Morgan despite the man's bluff attitude. There was not so much as a word between the two men as Grady left the house.

chapter 29

AFTER LEAVING MORGAN Grady Rogers walked two blocks to a corner drugstore and called a taxi. For a few moments his mind had been seething with angry thoughts. Then his customary calm returned to him.

Such a man, he thought. *Such a pompous, proud, hard, cruel human being. Reminds me of Nebuchadnezzar. "Whom he would he set up and whom he would he put down. But when his heart was lifted up and his mind hardened in pride he was deposed from his kingly throne." Who will depose this hard and cruel man who can't see justice for the hardness of his heart — who can't see mercy for the pride in his soul?*

The answer came at once. *Why God, of course. A God of justice and a God of mercy. He will see that righteousness prevails.*

The taxi arrived and Grady gave the bus depot as his destination. By riding all night he could catch the mail car to Clear Springs. There was much work to be done if Mary's Jody was to be saved for her. Grady was anxious to get started. He was worried, too, about Mrs. Goodman's condition. She was really seriously ill and might die suddenly at any time. He wanted to be handy to help if he could.

When he arrived in Clear Springs the next afternoon he found that she was much improved. She could even sit up in bed for short periods of time each day.

While he was away, Grady discovered, several things had happened. First of all, Mal had faced up to several facts that he had refused to recognize before. One was that he could not refuse to help a distressed young mother when he had the power to assist her. Another was that maybe Ann was right — maybe he was in love with Mary. Or maybe he just wanted to fall in love with her. Ever since Ann had mentioned it he had given Mary a great deal of thought. He found the thinking pleasant. Thirdly, and perhaps most important for his peace of mind, Mal realized that other men, too, had seen the horror and bloodshed in war just as he had and yet they had managed to retain their faith and their ideals and hopes.

Here's the way it had happened. After telling Grady that he would not defend Mary in the habeas corpus proceedings against her, Mal had thought to dismiss the whole thing from his mind. To his surprise, however, he discovered that he could not so easily erase it. Morning, noon and night his conscience kept hammering at him that he had no right to withhold this service that he could render because of his training and ability — not when someone like Mary was being pitifully imposed upon and had no weapons for her defense. After spending a few sleepless nights, Mal made up his mind to do what he could to defend Mary. Early one afternoon he started out to tell her of his decision.

He made his way slowly through the woods along the well-beaten path to the Goodman house. Though his leg had pretty well healed, he still had to be careful how he walked and used it. He left the path to wander down a tiny rivulet toward a spring. There he found it at the center of a grassy little dell, sweet smelling with the breath of spring flowers. There he also, surprisingly enough, found Mary with Jody playing nearby with his dog. (Grady had warned Mary not to let Jody out of her sight even for a moment for fear that he might be kidnapped).

The mother and child, were not alone, however. A tall, handsome young soldier with a boyish face was seated beside Mary on an old log near the spring. They were talking and laughing together animatedly. Mal noticed the crutch lying propped against the log beside the young man.

"Oh, Mr. Smith." Mary cried, springing up. "You — surprised — er — frightened me." She laughed in embarrassment.

"I'm sort of surprised myself," Mal returned. "I hope you will forgive me for the intrusion. I had no idea there was anyone down here."

"This is Frankie Jackson. And Frankie, this is Mr. Smith. I'm sure you have heard Brother Rogers or your mother speak of him."

"Indeed I have heard a lot about you, Frankie," Mal replied. "I'm happy to meet you."

"Same here," Frankie replied. "Mother and Dad talk a lot about you. And so does Mary here."

"She has no right to talk about me, because she doesn't know anything about me," Mal teased. From the half teasing, half reproachful look in his eye Mary could not tell whether he was serious or not.

"I know you busted a leg," Mary retorted. "I know, because I helped nurse you back to health and — and —" she hesitated.

"And what?" Mal grinned.

"And sanity," was the retort.

"You mean I was insane all those weeks? Why, Mary!"

"There were times when I wondered," Mary laughed. "but I suppose I was wrong. Just like the time I had to apologize for calling you pigheaded."

"Say, what goes on here?" Frankie broke in. "Don't you two get along?"

"We get along fine," Mary said. "Only I always open my mouth and say something crazy. Move over and let Mr. Smith sit here with us. He looks tired."

Mal was glad to sit. His leg had begun to pain him as a result of the exercising it had been given.

"I guess we've got a game leg apiece,"

Frankie began, "only yours is getting better and mine is hopeless."

"Hopeless! What do you mean?" Mary asked. "Isn't your leg going to be all right?"

"No, Mary, it isn't. I haven't told the folks yet, but I'm going to have to lose it. They're planning to amputate when I go back to the hospital. Then I'll have to stay there until I learn to use an artificial one before I can be discharged."

"But can't anything be done?" Mary said. "I thought with the new drugs and everything that they could do miraculous things."

"Many cures that seem almost miraculous are performed," Frankie stated simply, "but they can't seem to do anything in my case. They told me that they could prolong my amputation for several years perhaps. But those years would be filled with pain and suffering. And most of the time I'd be in the hospital."

Frankie paused momentarily, then went on, "I don't want to stay in a hospital that long. I've got a life to live — I've got work to do."

"Work? What kind of work?" Mal asked, wondering how a young man with such an ordeal facing him could look forward to life so eagerly.

"I'm going to be a preacher, sir. I made a covenant with God that if He would look after me during the war, that I'd give my life in service to Him. He surely kept His part of the bargain and now I'm going to keep mine."

"Seems like God wasn't looking after you

very well to let you lose a leg," Mal wanted to say. Mary half expected him to voice such a thought and broke in, "How will you train for the ministry, Frankie?" She already knew the answer for Frankie had told her of all of his plans before Mal joined them. Frankie had even told about the nurse in the hospital in San Diego whom he was going to marry. Mary thought, however, that it would do Mal good to hear Frank tell what he intended to do with his life.

"Just like I said, Mary," Frank answered, giving her a questioning glance, "I plan to go to the School of Religion at the University of Missouri. While I'm there I'd like to take some agricultural courses, too. I want to learn how to manage a farm for myself and be able to teach scientific farming methods. Then on Sundays and other times during the week I can devote myself to ministerial duties."

"Say, that sounds great," Mal responded, marvelling at his enthusiastic spirit. To think that he dared to attack all this hard work — with only one good leg. "Sounds reasonable and practical. Sounds like real religion too. The only thing is I wonder how you will manage your part of the farming — your own crops, I mean. Can you do it with just one leg?"

"I can buy a tractor with special levers and all that. A car, too, for that matter. Anyway I wouldn't plan for many row crops — mostly grass."

Mal nodded in agreement as Frankie went

on, "And I would try to arrange with some of the farmer members of my congregation to pay me in labor instead of money. That way it would be easier for them and it would do me just as much good too."

"I have one more question," Mal said. "It's kind of personal and perhaps I shouldn't ask it."

"Shoot," said Frankie. "My life is an open book. Isn't it, Mary?" And he looked at her fondly — too fondly Mal thought and flushed uncomfortably.

Mary paid no heed to either of them but only listened for Mal's question.

"How will you finance your education? Do you have savings for that?"

"Yes, partly at least," Frankie answered. "Every month I was in the service I sent $50 to Mom to put away for me. Each month she and Uncle Dave added $15 or $20 to it. Now altogether I have nearly $2,000. That will not be enough to see me through all the plans I have, but it'll help an awful lot. I'll get through all right — the Lord will see to that!" At this point Frankie winked at Mary. Mal felt as though he had been hit with a truck. *They must be planning to get married,* he thought. *No wonder she looks so fresh and pretty today, sitting here giving him such rapt attention.*

"Of course He will, Frankie," Mary said fondly. "Don't you think so, Mr. Smith?"

"You shouldn't ask a question like that of a man who hasn't any faith," Mal teased.

"Oh, but that's not true. You do have faith. When you plant seeds in the ground, you expect them to come up and grow and mature, don't you? That's faith. You wandered off down here to the spring to smell the sweet fragrance of the flowers because you knew how lovely they would be here in this beautiful spot, didn't you? Isn't that some kind of faith?"

Mal knew how right she was — how right she always seemed to be. Throughout the long winter months he had kept in his mind a vision of how lovely this little glen would be in the spring.

Almost daily since the first warm days had come and before he could leave the house, he had asked Grady and Rosie and others who came to tell him about the flowers. He hadn't cared much for the bouquets of violets and buttercups that Grady had carried to the house. *Wild flowers should be left where they are,* he thought. But, oh how he had longed to wander through the woods to find them growing shyly and bravely round the stumps and in the dells.

Of course, Mal had never voiced any of these inner feelings to anyone. He was shy, too. Shy as the violets he dreamed about. And, too, he had grievances to nurse. A man that was doing everything in his power to forget the painful things of life — things that should have brought joy, like flowers or anniversaries, a mother's comforting good-night kiss, the sweet, tender caresses of a woman — he doesn't like to admit he is beginning to enjoy life again, even to himself.

"I suppose one can't completely lose his faith, then, can he?" Mal asked slowly. "I think Brother Rogers has been trying to tell me that for a long time."

"No, but he can sure find times when it wears awfully thin," Frankie said seriously.

"Why, Frankie, surely not you," Mary gasped.

"Mary, 'War is hell' just like Sherman said. When one gets mixed up in all of that killing and pain and loneliness and hatred it is hard to believe at the same time that anything good exists. For some people I guess it's impossible."

"But you didn't lose your faith," Mary insisted.

"I had a mother writing to me, praying for me, believing in me. Then, too, I realized that I had to cast my all on the Lord — and He is faithful! And Mother — she believes that when the faith of one she loves is weak then her strength must be great enough for both."

"Oh, Rosie," Mary said almost reverently. "Hers is a love that will not let you go. Something like God's love for all of us. Only His love is so much greater."

Mal remembered what Grady had told him about Rosie's unwavering faith when Hiram was a fugitive from the law for four years. He could not help thinking, too, of that beautiful hymn "Oh,

Love That Wilt Not Let Me Go." It had always been one of his favorites.

"Yes, I suppose it would be different if a man had a wife or mother like that at home waiting for him, believing in him," he said simply.

Mary glanced at her watch. "Oh my!" she exclaimed. "I must go. I had no idea it was so late."

"Come Jody," she called to the child, now happily wading in the stream picking flowers while the adults talked nearby.

"I'd better get back too," Frank laughed, "or Mother will come looking for me. She will hardly let me out of her sight."

"I don't blame her," Mary smiled. "And please tell her not to worry about Mother while you are here. She's getting so much better now."

"I'm glad," Frank replied looking at her again so fondly that Mal winced. Then he turned to Mal and said, "Goodbye, Mr. Smith. I'm glad to have met you. This has been a pleasant afternoon."

"Indeed it has," Mal answered. "I wish you the very best of everything. You deserve it."

"Goodbye, Frank. Come over and see us," Mary sang out gaily, in a very unlover-like way Mal thought. Then she turned with Jody toward the path that would take her home.

"Oh, Miss Goodman," Mal called, "I had started over to your house to see you when I got this far." Mal hobbled slowly toward her.

Mary stopped and waited for him to catch up with her. "To tell the truth," she said, "I had started to your house to see you, too, but I got scared and went over to the spring to think things over. It's a favorite spot of mine."

"Mine, too. I've dreamed all winter of finding it just like it was today," Mal said. "But why did you get scared?"

"Oh, I'm so worried about losing — about the case that is coming up against me," she spoke softly so that Jody wouldn't hear. "I wanted to ask you to help me. Brother Rogers thought you might. Then I just couldn't bring myself to ask you to take part in something like this when you have no interest in it."

"But I find I do have an interest in this case. I have interest in seeing justice done. And I have an interest in you and Jody," Mal said honestly. "I had just come to tell you that I would defend you if you wanted me to."

"Oh, thank you. You don't know what this means to me." Tears filled Mary's eyes. "It looked like I'm going to lose everything. Mother, Jody — how could I stand to lose him?"

Exactly what Ann said to me — almost, Mal thought forlornly. To Mary he said gently, "Don't cry. I'll do the best for you that I can. Grady Rogers may have some good news for us when he returns."

"I wish I could tell you all about Jody." The child and his dog were far enough away so that she spoke normally. "It would make such a difference. But I'm not free to tell."

"Ann has already told me," Mal said simply.

"Ann!" Mary ejaculated. "Why, I don't understand. Ann would never tell. Not as long as mother lives she wouldn't."

"Ann told me," Mal repeated. "And when the time comes you must give it as evidence if necessary. You or Ann, one or the other."

"No! No! Never!" Mary cried.

"It may be the only way you can save Jody."

"It's a chance I'll have to take," Mary said quietly, sighing deeply.

"You wouldn't perjure yourself," Mal said.

Mary was aghast. "You wouldn't make me tell," she gasped. "Surely, you wouldn't do that. It would kill Mother!"

"I suppose not," Mal said. "Not if you feel so strongly about it. But it seems to me that what is best for Jody should be the prime factor in this case no matter who else gets hurt."

"It's strange you would think of that when you have no interest in the affairs of others," Mary thrust at him, ashamed that her duty to Jody above everything else had been pointed out to her.

"I'm beginning to have a great deal of concern about what happens to some of the people I know," Mal returned. "And now that I have taken your case, I have a great deal of studying to do.

I may have to be gone for a few days. But don't worry, I'll be back in time for the trial."

"I am so grateful I don't know what to say. I hope someday I can do something for you to show my gratitude."

Mal did not reply, he only looked at her in a searching sort of way. Mary felt suddenly uncomfortable. Then he glanced up where Jody was romping with his dog in the grass. "Keep him near you every minute. We don't want him snatched from you."

Then Mal turned to walk away, leaving Mary looking after him with a queer sort of ache in her heart — an ache strangely tied up with the limping man.

When Mal had taken not more than twenty slow tedious steps, he turned and came back to her.

"There is one thing I must know," he said abruptly. "Are you going to marry Frank Jackson?"

Mary couldn't have been more surprised. "Of course not," she answered quickly. "Why do you ask?"

Mal was surprised at his own relief at her answer.

"I don't know," he said feeling a little foolish. "It just looked like maybe you were when you were talking together this afternoon. Some of the things you said. I thought you both looked at each other rather fondly."

"I am fond of Frankie," Mary admitted.

"We grew up together. But I'm four years older than he is."

"Does difference in age have something to do with the way you care for a man?" Mal inquired.

"No, I suppose not necessarily. But Frankie and I are only good friends. He is going to marry a nurse he met in San Diego. He told me all about it."

"Oh, I see," Mal said inadequately. "Well, keep an eye on Jody and I'll see you again soon."

Again he turned from her but this time Mary didn't stare after him. She was too much mystified by his behavior for that. Puzzled and in a vague way sort of happy, she walked through the coolness of the woods toward home with Jody beside her.

Oh, Jody, Jody, I can't let them have you, she thought as she hugged him close to her before kissing him goodnight. *Surely God and Mal will find a way for me to keep you.*

chapter 30

CHARACTERISTICALLY, once having decided to defend Mary in her case to keep custody of Jody, Mal set to work determinedly to prepare the best case possible for her. He had already hired a young man in the community to do his chores until he was fully able again. When he reached home, therefore, all he had to do was to set his supper on the table and eat before he was ready to begin work on the case.

Mal had not intended to keep his statute books with him when he moved his belongings. He deliberately left them because he did not intend to practice law again and thought he would not need them. His law partner, however, when he disposed of Mal's goods for him, crated the book boxes and shipped them to Mal without asking him anything about it. Mal was irritated when they arrived but had moved them into the house where he left them pushed against a wall in the bedroom. He had not bothered to unpack them.

Mal unpacked the boxes until he found the volumes he particularly needed. Then with pencil and paper he sat down to study and take notes. Somehow he found it hard to concentrate. The words of the hymn kept drumming in his brain. They were mixed up with the conversation

he had had with Mary and Frank in the afternoon.
Mary's sweet face came between him and the
pages he was reading. Ann's accusation, Jody, Frank
Jackson, Grady Rogers, Mr. Morgan. Where did
they all fit in the scheme of things? They all had
plans — plans they intended to work out. *I don't
seem to fit in with anything*, Mal thought. Then
the words returned —

> O love that wilt not let me go
> I rest my weary soul in Thee;
> I give Thee back the life I owe . . .

Mal dropped his pencil and strode out
to the porch, "*I give Thee back the life I owe*," he
mused. *That's what makes all of them so happy
— Rosie, Mary, Frankie, Grady — they have given
their lives back to God. I, too, must find my way
back. I once was close to God — I must find Him
again.*

"But how!" he cried out then in anguish.
"Where are You, God, that I can't seem to reach
You?"

Then he thought of Grady Rogers and the
story the preacher had told of how he had to
go out and search for God the night his little boy,
Tommy, died.

"I didn't want to let Tommy go," Grady
had said, "although I knew in my soul it was God's
will. I knew it was best for Tommy, too. But I
had to seek peace with God before I could let him
go."

Without knowing why, Mal left his home

and struck out over the path that Grady had traveled that long night years before. Only Mal's going was slow and painstaking because of his leg. He had to stop and rest many times on the weary mountainous climb. He had to get off where he could think — and analyze what was happening to him. A peace he hadn't known for years was beginning to envelop him. God seemed near again.

Mal knew the way because Grady had taken him there when he told him the story. It was a beautiful spot, but the story had frightened him.

Mal had never gone back to the place. Not until tonight. Now he could not stay away. Grady had found God there. Now Mal wanted to be alone with God there himself. He felt clean and washed as he drew near.

At last the long, hard climb was over and Mal, weary and spent, hobbled across the shelf of land that towered high above a beautiful green valley just as the dawn was chasing away the shaddows of the night. The rising sun cast a pink glow over the clouds that hovered near the horizon.

The glory of God shines all about, Mal thought as he dropped wearily upon a rock to rest. Too tired to sit up he lay prone upon the ground and closed his eyes. "Lord," he whispered prayerfully. "You are surely in this place. I thank Thee for showing me the way back to You."

As he lay there quietly resting the words of Psalm 139 — "If I take the wings of the morning and dwell in the uttermost parts of the sea; even there shall Thy hand lead me and Thy right hand shall hold me" — began to repeat themselves in his mind.

Mal did not know why he thought of those words. Only God knew that. But it was just what he needed to help him now. "On every flight while I was in the war those words gave me the courage I had to have," he exulted. "I did dwell in the uttermost parts and God cared for me. God still cares," he almost shouted, "He cares and I care."

Mal rose from the ground and walking to the edge of the cliff threw open his arms and cried aloud, "Peace! Peace! Peace at last in my soul and it has come on the wings of the dawn!"

He turned and hurried down the mountains heedless of his injured leg. When he reached home he fell into bed without any breakfast. He slept until noon. Then he got up, shaved and ate a hearty lunch.

After eating Mal sat down at the piano for the first time since before his injury and played rapturously. When Grady Rogers approached the house, he could scarcely believe his ears. Mal was singing in as fine a bass voice as Grady had ever heard that favorite hymn, "O Love That Wilt Not Let Me Go."

Grady knew as soon as he entered the room and caught a glimpse of Mal's face what had happened to him. He dropped into an easy chair and listened while Mal finished the song. Then he said,

"Only when a man has made peace with God does he have that look on his face. Do you want to tell me about it?"

"No, Grady, if you don't mind. It's just too new and precious to me now to talk about it. But it's real and genuine and you'll not find me wandering away again."

"I'm glad, Mal," Grady said simply. "I prayed that this would happen. Now may God bless you and use you."

"Just this one thing, Grady," Mal said, "I want you to know that now I can pray. Do you have any idea of the anguish in a man's soul who can't pray?"

"I've seen it in other men's lives. Thank God, I've never had the experience. I try to live honestly with myself and all men. When I need God I can reach out for Him and He is there."

"What a blessing," Mal said reverently as he moved toward the desk where his law books lay.

Grady noticed the books and looked questioningly at Mal. "I decided to take the case," Mal said by way of explanation. "Tell me what you learned."

Step by step Grady went over his visit with F. Monroe Morgan with Mal.

"Hmmm," Mal commented when he had finished, "he sounds rather unpleasant. But I don't believe he can win his case. It is hard to take a child from his parent."

"By fair means, maybe," Grady pointed out. "But suppose they play foul?"

"That could easily happen," Mal answered, "but we hope not. At least we know the kind of man we're dealing with. You did a good job, Grady."

"I haven't solved anything for Mary," Grady said wearily. "Do you know how her mother is?"

"Much better. They are hopeful now that she may be up and around again."

"That's good. It will make the going easier for the girls when the trial comes. And now that I've told you about the trip, I think I'll run along. I'm awfully tired. These hills surely do look good after a few days in the city."

"They look good anytime," Mal replied, following his visitor to the door. "Goodbye, Grady. After you've rested a day or two I'll want to see you again. In the meantime I'll have a lot of studying to do."

Mal plunged into the case wholeheartedly. Night and day he read and studied to prepare a brief.

Five days before the trial he left the area. No one knew where he had gone. He was working with the young attorney whom he had earlier contacted in Springfield. The two of them made trips to several points to make contacts. Mal was glad for a partner who could do the driving while his leg still needed coddling.

The day he was ready to come home, however, Mal went to an auto agency and purchased a new car. After driving home the day before the hearing, he asked Grady Rogers to tell Mary he wanted to see her. He requested that she come to his home. (Mal made it a point to stay away from the Goodman home. He did not want to encounter Ann.)

It was then that Grady told Mal about Mrs. Goodman's reaction when she heard about the efforts to take Jody. The shock had caused a relapse and nervous collapse. She was much worse than she had ever been and had been taken to the hospital in Hartstown. The girls were there with her.

"Then I'll go to Hartstown," Mal said. "I must see Mary before tomorrow. Do you want to come along?"

Grady went. On the way he asked, "What are your chances to win, Mal?"

"Not good in this court," the lawyer said, "If we lose tomorrow, we can, of course, take it to a court of appeals. It can well be a different story there."

"Mal, you told me once that you had information that made it impossible for you to take this case. Then when I came back you made a different decision. What made you change your mind? Did you find you could use the information after all?"

"I wish I could," Mal responded, "but I

can't. However, someone else can if they choose and maybe they will. I keep hoping so!

"I guess several things made me change my mind," he continued. "I guess once a lawyer, always a lawyer. Anyway I felt wretchedly guilty to stand idly by doing nothing to help Mary while the child was being taken from her just like a doctor might have felt to have refused aid to someone in need.

"Then too, the injustice of it all sort of riles me. Mary can do more for Jody than anyone else and she should have him."

They had arrived at the hospital by this time. Mal went in to see Mary. He had hoped she could go for a ride with him, but she would not leave her mother. Mal did not mention his new car. He briefed the case for her in as short time as possible and told her not to worry.

Looking at her careworn face, Mal wanted to pick Mary up in his arms and carry her off to a place of safety where no more of these things could reach her — a place where they could talk and he could tell her of the wonderful thing that had happened to him on top of the mountain.

Instead he gave her some routine instructions and sent her back to her dying mother. Then, each occupied with his own thinking, he and Grady drove silently home through the gathering dusk.

chapter 31

Most of the Clear Springs people were already in the courtroom when Mal and Grady arrived with Mary Goodman. Hiram and Rosie were there with four-year-old Jody. The boy was looking around him with absent-minded interest. Mary had not permitted anyone to talk to him about what was taking place, although she herself had explained to him that they would have to answer a lot of questions and that there would be lots of people. Jody seemed satisfied and exhibited little concern.

Just as the court house clock began to strike the hour of ten, Mal and Mary walked with the little boy down the aisle to the counsel table. The bailiff called the court room to order just before the judge entered the room. He slowly turned the docket pages and called the case by name and number.

Grady Rogers recognized Mr. Morgan amply flanked by a cortege of attorneys. That pompous personage paid no attention to anyone in the courtroom except his lawyers. He kept pulling out his watch and seemed anxious to get on with the proceedings.

"Are all parties ready for trial?" the judge finally asked.

273

Both the plaintiff and the defense stated that they were.

"Each side may have fifteen minutes to present a summary of its case. Plaintiff may proceed," the judge barked routinely.

Mr. Morgan's lawyer arose and spent ten minutes extolling the virtues of his client. Then he said they proposed to show convincing evidence that the defendant was an ambitious young woman, a gold digger, social climber and of questionable reputation; that she had used her powers as a woman to ensnare this fine young soldier, a son of a wealthy and influential father, into marriage taking advantage of his youth, loneliness and innocence of the ways of worldly women. That such a woman was qualified to care for a child he declared highly questionable.

"I am sure when all of the evidence has been presented the court can return no decision except for my client who, by every reasonable argument, should have custody of this sweet child," he concluded.

Mal spoke for only ten minutes. He eloquently pleaded for the court to render a verdict of justice in favor of the mother retaining custody of her child. He told of Mary's virtues as a woman and a mother, of her impeccable reputation in the community, of her many kindnesses and devotion to her mother.

"This mother is in every way the proper person to rear this child. And she is in a position to match advantages for him with those claimed by the plaintiff. She can give him everything the child needs to make him a happy, useful citizen. Not wealth and power and social prominence perhaps," Mal emphasized each of these three qualifications in a pointed way, "but proper physical care, proper housing, good food, education, religious and cultural training — and what is perhaps more important than all of these, the security that comes from the knowledge a child has of a mother's abiding and unselfish love.

"Can Mr. Morgan offer this child Jody all of these things? The answer is 'no.' When the evidence is all in this court can only decide for the defendant."

Mal sat beside Mary and Jody at the counsel table as the hearing proceeded.

The plaintiff called the first witness, Mary. The usual routine questions were asked and Mary answered clearly and distinctly giving her name, age, place of residence, occupation and other information.

Mal knew what the next question probably would be and wondered what Mary would do about it. He had warned her at all costs to tell the truth.

"Were you at one time married to the defendant's son?" the lawyer questioned.

"Yes," Mary answered calmly. She then proceeded to answer when and where she was married.

"How long were you married before your husband went overseas?" was the next question.

"Two weeks," was the prompt answer.

"In what month was this?"

"March."

"In what month was Jody born?"

"September," Mary answered, miserable as she noticed the knowing looks on the faces about her.

"Then you were pregnant when you married Mr. Morgan's son," the attorney pounced.

"No! No! I don't know," Mary cried knowing she was trapped.

"You don't know! You are the child's mother, aren't you?" the man was relentless.

Mary opened her mouth to speak and then closed it again. She looked appealingly at Mal, but he appeared not to be listening to what was going on at all.

The attorney evidently sensed that something was decidedly wrong, as did most of the audience.

"I asked you a question, Mrs. Morgan. Will you kindly answer? Are you the mother of this child?"

"No," Mary answered simply. "No, I'm not."

No answer could have created greater consternation. The spectators sat forward in their seats. The plaintiff's attorney was at a complete loss as he saw the whole case crumpling before him.

"If you are not the mother of this child, then

who is?" the bewildered man asked lamely.

Ann Goodman had entered the crowded courtroom, but in the general excitement no one had paid any attention to her.

When she heard the question put to Mary she moved quickly forward. Reaching the front of the room she stated clearly, "I am Jody's mother." An electrifying silence followed this confession. Then the courtroom was thrown into an uproar.

The judge pounded furiously with his gavel before order was finally restored. The plaintiff and his lawyers were alternately shaking their heads and mopping their brows. Grady was trying to put the pieces of this jigsaw puzzle together. Mary sat aghast in the witness chair and Jody had run over and hidden his head in her lap. The only two persons who seemed to possess their self-control were Mal and Ann, who had seated herself at the counsel table and waited to finish the trying ordeal.

When the room was once more quiet, Mal rose from his chair and approached the bench.

"Your honor," he said, "at this time I wish to ask the court to dismiss this action in habeas corpus on the premise that these defendants are not the proper defendants and their petition is of no force and effect."

The judge studied the petition that Mal handed him for a moment. Then he raised his head to state, "I assume you are in a position to prove that this young woman is not the mother of this child."

"I am, your honor. I have documentary evidence," Mal answered.

"Then court will be recessed for an hour," the judge ordered, "while we straighten out this tangled mess." Then the judge, the attorneys, the plaintiff and Mary retired to the judge's private chambers.

Ann sat white faced and tense while she waited. Her back was to the audience and she kept it that way. People eyed her curiously as they filed from the courtroom. Only Rosie came forward to speak to her and ask if she wanted anything.

"Nothing at all, Rosie, thank you," Ann replied.

"Then may I take Jody out for a little walk and something to eat?" Rosie asked.

"It will be best for him," Ann agreed.

When the court was reconvened the judge ruled "Case Dismissed." The court was adjourned for the day.

As soon as Mary was free to move she ran to Ann. "Oh, Ann," she said, "why did you do it? Think of Mother!"

"Mary," Ann replied, "it won't bother Mother. She's gone. Just before I came here she closed her eyes and went away. Nothing will ever hurt her now. Now I'm going away, too. You can take care of things here. You won't need me. You have Grady Rogers and Rosie and worlds of friends — and Mal Smith."

"What about Jody?" Mary wanted to know.

She had not yet grasped the meaning of Ann's words concerning Mrs. Goodman.

"I've no right to Jody," Ann answered. "You know that. He is really yours. Today has been bad for him, but he will soon forget. Goodbye now. I hope you won't mind that I am taking the car to Springfield. I'll leave it there and you can get it later."

"But Ann, where are you going?"

"I'll write you when I get settled. I never expect to return to this place, but I'll want to hear about Jody. Goodbye, Mary."

Ann was gone before anyone but Mary realized what had happened. But the news of their mother's death had reached the courtroom. Rosie and Grady Rogers bore the news to her and quietly eased her away through a side exit.

chapter 32

THE REACTION OF THOSE who had come to hear the trial was quite normal. Everyone made accusations and, of course, nearly every person who expressed an opinion was quick to judge Ann. Sympathy was lavished on Mary.

Rosie stayed close to Mary's side. They left the courtroom and went at once to the hospital. There Mary learned from the nurses of her mother's last moments. The body had already been moved to the funeral home at her sister's orders.

The funeral for Mrs. Goodman, too, was conducted according to the custom of this Ozark region. Grady Rogers was to take charge of the burial services the next afternoon at two o'clock. Hiram Jackson took care of opening the grave next to Mr. Goodman's. Neighbors came with boxes of food to sit with Mary all through the long night and through the next day till the hour of the funeral.

After all that kind friends could do was done and Mary's mother was placed in the earth alongside her husband, Mary and Jody went home with Rosie to rest for a few days.

With the beginning of warm weather Mal and Grady both decided to meet for their evening meals at Mrs. Morgan's boarding house. Several vacationers were coming into the region again for the fishing season and Mrs. Morgan had built some small cabins for tourist accommodations. She also furnished meals for those using the cabins, among whom were two ladies.

They wore modern outdoor clothing, much to Mrs. Morgan's disgust, but she enjoyed visiting with them nonetheless. She kept everyone informed on all neighborhood happenings.

The ladies and men alike were interested in her account of the trial and Mrs. Goodman's death.

"And there we all were," she recounted, "a sittin' on pins wondering what Mary meant when she said she wasn't the mother. Then in walked Ann bold as brass and said smart as you please that she was Jody's mother."

"I suppose it was a great shock to everyone," a guest responded.

"Humph," their narrator sniffed, "with all that reddish-like hair, whose child did they think it was? I never did think much of those girls.

"But I guess I was always a little wrong about Mary, though. She seemed real sad at her mother's funeral," she continued. "Seems like things is going to be awful lonely for her now."

Mal at his table was beginning to feel somewhat uncomfortable that Mary's private affairs were being so thoroughly aired. To change the topic of conversation he began asking the guests about their day's fishing. Grady too, relieved at the turn of the

conversation, helped him out. Soon the happenings
of the community were forgotten.

Ever since her mother's death Mal had felt
a protective interest in Mary. Still he felt himself
to be too much of a stranger to offer help in the
hours that followed when her grief was young. *This
is a time when her intimate friends who have
known her all her life should be with her,* he
reasoned.

He sent a huge spray of flowers, more elabor-
ate than those of anyone else, and he also went
to the funeral. For the rest of the time, however,
he stayed away from her, although his heart and
mind were filled with thoughts of nothing else.

Several days after Mrs. Goodman's funeral
Mal talked to Grady of the way he felt toward
Mary.

"Are you in love with her?" Grady asked.

"I don't know," Mal replied. "The idea that
I'd ever fall in love again seems so preposterous.
Anyway, Mary sort of scares me."

"Scares you!" Grady exclaimed. "Quiet, gentle Mary Goodman shouldn't frighten a man."

"Perhaps you haven't ever noticed," Mal
responded, "that Mary is quiet and reserved only
when in the presence of Ann. When she is with
others she seems to be just the opposite—a gay,
laughing girl."

"Oh, yes," Grady said, "everyone who has
known Mary for a long time knows that to be
true."

"Ann must have been really very unkind to her."

"It isn't that so much," Grady explained, "as the fact that she was always made to feel, especially by her mother, that Ann was smarter and much the prettier of the two. It gave Mary a complex."

"Maybe she will be able to overcome it now," Mal said hopefully.

"I'm sure she will. And if I were you, my friend, I would ask her to go out with me. A little social life and relaxation would be fine for her."

"Grady, I'm a very shy man," Mal confessed, drawing a long sigh. "Always have been and am worse than ever now. Will you do me a great favor? Will you ask Mary to go out with me?"

"Mal," Grady laughed, "I've been asked to do a lot of unusual things in my life time, but this is the first time I've ever been asked to play the role of John Alden."

"And you are not being asked that now," his friend reminded him. "I didn't say to ask her to marry me. Only to go out with me."

"I'll see her first thing tomorrow," Grady agreed. "I'll let you know."

The next morning Grady went by the Jackson's home on his way to the post office. Only Mary was at home. Hiram was in the fields and the rest of the family were working at the store and post office.

When Grady gave her his message she was a little flustered. Grady could see that she had more than a passing interest in Mal. She finally agreed to go out with Mal if he drove by for her that evening after supper.

"Rosie has been telling me that Mr. Smith — Mal — would sooner or later ask me to go out with him but I didn't believe it," Mary said. "I've been feeling very lonely. It'll be good to get away for a few hours."

"Mal is lonely too," Grady said. "An evening together will be good for both of you."

Mal arrived at five o'clock that evening neatly dressed in an expertly tailored suit. Mary had never seen him looking more distinguished and handsome. She, too, was ready in a new spring suit, her hair brushed until it curled invitingly about her gentle face.

Rosie loaned Mary her new purse and gloves and Frankie whistled at her as she passed by him on her way from the bedroom to the front porch.

Hiram did not say anything about how nice Mary looked but he listened with interest while the family gave an excited account of Mary's date with Mal. The little girls and Frankie exchanged winks when they saw their father walk awkwardly up behind Rosie as she stood at the stove and whirl her around to kiss her.

Mary had just finished dressing and was sitting on the porch when Mal drove up in front of the house. She looked at her watch and said, "Why, it's only five o'clock! I thought you were coming after supper."

"You seem to be ready. I thought we could go to Hartstown for dinner," Mal suggested, a little uncomfortable in his finery. He could not understand how he had failed to see how lovely Mary was before. He felt almost tongue-tied in her presence.

Mary was delighted with the idea. "If Rosie doesn't mind I'd love to," she said considerately. "She was planning for me to eat with them."

Rosie told Mary to run along and to have a good time. As the car drove down the dusty lane its occupants were curiously watched by every pair of eyes in Rosie's house.

The evening was all too short for both of them. When they had returned from Hartstown after several hours of happy companionship and were sitting for a few moments in the car Mal said thoughtfully, "You know, I believe Ann was right. She told me I was in love with you."

"Ann shouldn't have said that," Mary gasped.

"I'm glad she did," Mal replied. "The strange thing about it is that it's true. I just never realized it before. The question is how do you feel? About me I mean?"

"I don't know," Mary said. "I haven't had any right to think anything."

"I want you to think about it," Mal pleaded.

"Think about it all of the time from now on until you're sure."

"After tonight I'm sure I will be thinking about you a lot, Mal. We'll discover before long if Ann was right."

"But before we do there are some things I want to talk about with you. You know about me and Kathy, but there is an obligation I haven't told you about. When can I see you again?"

"A picnic tomorrow would be nice," Mary suggested.

"Wonderful," Mal agreed. "Where?"

"Why not the little glen at the spring?"

"My favorite spot!" Mal said delightedly.

"Mine too. I'll meet you there with a basket of lunch at noon tomorrow."

"It's a date," Mal said boyishly. Then he opened the door of the car and walked with her to the porch where they said good night.

The next day Mal was too impatient to wait until noon and wandered down to the spring at eleven o'clock. Mary found him there soon after. After a satisfying lunch they sat in the grass and talked the afternoon away, telling each other the little things about themselves that lovers will. They shared the experiences of their childhood and youth. Each learned of the other's ambitions, ideals and aspirations. They talked at length of each other's marriages. They felt that they should be completely honest and fair with each other about their respective pasts.

Mal told Mary how he had gone to visit Kathy while investigating Jody's case in the northern part of the state. She was hopelessly ill in a sanitarium.

"Something impelled me to go," he said. "I wanted to know for sure how I felt about her."

"What did you find?" Mary asked quietly.

"Only pity for her," Mal replied. "Pity and compassion. She can never be any better and she knows it. She asked if I had come for her little girl, Gloria, and I told her I had."

"And what did she say to that?" Mary wanted to know.

" 'Then I can die in peace,' " Mal quoted.

"The poor thing," Mary sympathized, thinking how tragic for a woman to lose the love of a man like Mal. "I, too, can only pity her." She wiped the tears from her eyes. "And where is Gloria now?"

"Judge Dalton has been paying for her care in a private home. Now I shall assume that obligation. I made application to adopt her."

"Oh, Mal, let me have her," Mary asked. "She can grow up to play with Jody. He needs a companion."

"It will mean a lot to me if you are sure you want to take on that much responsibility," Mal said.

To which Mary replied, "I'm quite sure. Is it all settled?"

"That much is," Mal answered as he rose to his feet and pulled Mary up to him.

"There is this one thing more though, Mary. I have never believed in divorce. My separation from Kathy was forced upon me just as I have told you. As long as Kathy lives I shall not feel free to marry, but some day, my dear, when I am free I am going to ask you to be my wife. In the meantime try to have an answer ready."

"I'll be ready, Mal," Mary answered softly.

Mary and Mal had to wait nearly two years before they were married. When Gloria came Mary took her in as her own. The little girl soon came to call her "mother" and to think of Jody as her big brother. Mal was "Unca Mal." That was changed to "Daddy" when Mary and Mal were married. Mal bought out Ann's part in the Goodman farm and the two farms were combined to form a ranch as Mal had hoped.

Ann, true to her resolution, never returned to Clear Springs. She became a nurse in a large hospital in California.

Frankie Jackson married his nurse and went through the state university in preparation for his work in Clear Springs. Knowing that Grady Rogers would soon retire, he wanted to be ready.

Mal and Mary often stand on their porch and watch the sun rise over the mountains. They are thankful for what those mountains have meant to them, the peace and the quietness that have come. God has been good, and they are glad.